## Keeping Up Appearances

"Of course I've had sex," she told him. "But we're not talking about me. We're talking about your reputation with the ladies."

"I didn't know I had a reputation with the ladies," he said.

"You think all people talk about is how fast the Gunsmith is with a gun?" she asked. "Then you haven't heard your own stories, have you?"

"To tell you the truth, I try not to listen to them," he told her.

"Well, believe me," she said, "that reputation is considerable." She leaned forward, placed her elbows on the table, and lowered her voice. "In fact, that's the one I'm interested in right now."

"Are you telling me that's what you want to interview me about?" he asked.

"Actually," she said, touching the back of his hand, "I was thinking about . . . research."

D0681018

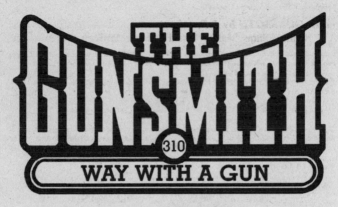

# THE GUNSMITH

### 310

## WAY WITH A GUN

## J. R. ROBERTS

JOVE BOOKS, NEW YORK

**THE BERKLEY PUBLISHING GROUP**
**Published by the Penguin Group**
**Penguin Group (USA) Inc.**
**375 Hudson Street, New York, New York 10014, USA**
Penguin Group (Canada), 90 Eglinton Avenue East, Suite 700, Toronto, Ontario M4P 2Y3, Canada
(a division of Pearson Penguin Canada Inc.)
Penguin Books Ltd., 80 Strand, London WC2R 0RL, England
Penguin Group Ireland, 25 St. Stephen's Green, Dublin 2, Ireland (a division of Penguin Books Ltd.)
Penguin Group (Australia), 250 Camberwell Road, Camberwell, Victoria 3124, Australia
(a division of Pearson Australia Group Pty. Ltd.)
Penguin Books India Pvt. Ltd., 11 Community Centre, Panchsheel Park, New Delhi—110 017, India
Penguin Group (NZ), 67 Apollo Drive, Rosedale, North Shore 0745, Auckland, New Zealand
(a division of Pearson New Zealand Ltd.)
Penguin Books (South Africa) (Pty.) Ltd., 24 Sturdee Avenue, Rosebank, Johannesburg 2196,
South Africa

Penguin Books Ltd., Registered Offices: 80 Strand, London WC2R 0RL, England

This is a work of fiction. Names, characters, places, and incidents either are the product of the author's imagination or are used fictitiously, and any resemblance to actual persons, living or dead, business establishments, events, or locales is entirely coincidental.

WAY WITH A GUN

A Jove Book / published by arrangement with the author

PRINTING HISTORY
Jove edition / October 2007

Copyright © 2007 by Robert J. Randisi.
Cover illustration by Sergio Giovine.

ISBN: 978-0-515-14361-4

JOVE®
Jove Books are published by The Berkley Publishing Group,
a division of Penguin Group (USA) Inc.,
375 Hudson Street, New York, New York 10014.
JOVE is a registered trademark of Penguin Group (USA) Inc.
The "J" design is a trademark belonging to Penguin Group (USA) Inc.

PRINTED IN THE UNITED STATES OF AMERICA

10 9 8 7 6 5 4 3 2 1

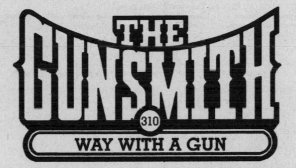

# THE GUNSMITH

### 310

## WAY WITH A GUN

# ONE

.

Tell Barlow stared across the table at his two colleagues. Jerry Corbett was in his early thirties, the youngest of the three men. He somehow always managed to look like he was fresh-shaven. Newly Yates was the oldest, in his early forties, and always had a dark stubble growing around a toothpick.

Tell was thirty-five, dressed better than the other two, who always seemed to be in trail clothes—Corbett's clean, Newly's dirty. The other two were like night and day, with Tell somewhere in the middle. The one thing they all had in common was that they made their way with a gun. There were no two ways about it, these men were killers. They did it well, and for money.

But they had something else in common too.

They were bored with their lives.

They were in the Five Aces saloon in Selkirk, Arizona. There was no one else in the place except for the bartender. That was because these three men, just by their presence, scared away other patrons, who preferred to drink somewhere else while they were in town.

Tell, Newly, and Corbett were playing poker and talking about how bored they were.

1

"Let's raise the stakes," Newly said.

"What for?" Tell asked. "We all charge a lot for our services. We should all have enough money put away that we wouldn't even have to work if we didn't want to."

Newly and Corbett looked at each other.

"Well, *I* do," Tell said. "Raising the stakes of a god-damned poker game ain't gonna make no difference to me."

"Then what will?" Corbett asked.

"I don't know." Tell threw his cards down on the table. "Somethin' that'll make a difference."

"Like what?" Newly asked.

Tell slid his chair back angrily and said, "Jesus, can't you fellas come up with anything but questions? I'm gettin' another beer."

"Can I get one?" Newly asked.

"Me too," Corbett said.

"Jesus . . ."

Tell went to the bar and told the bartender to let him have three more beers.

"And make these cold ones," he added.

"Yessir."

Tell was disgusted with his life. His last half-dozen jobs had been so easy it was laughable. He wanted to feel challenged. All he had to do was figure out how.

When he got back to the table, Newly was cackling, have just taken a hand from Corbett. Tell pushed their beers at them, spilling some of each on the table.

"Hey!" Newly said. He grabbed the cards before they could get soaked with beer.

"Think of somethin', damn it!" Tell said.

"Jesus, Tell," Corbett said, "what the hell . . ."

"How good are you with a gun, Newly?"

"Damned good."

"Fast?"

"Not fast, but I hit what I aim at."

"I'm fast," Corbett said.

"How fast?" Tell asked.

"Faster than you."

"You sure?"

Corbett hesitated, then said, "Yeah," in a less-than-confident voice.

"Sure enough to bet?"

"Bet what?"

"That you can outdraw me."

"I mean, what are we bettin'?"

"Whatever," Tell said. "Money? Horses? How about your life?"

"My life?" Corbett asked.

"Our lives," Tell said. "You against me. Winner takes all. Loser dies."

"That's crazy, Tell," Newly said.

"It'd be interestin'," Tell said.

"Crazy interestin'," Newly said. "Why don't you find some other way to find out who's faster?"

"Like what?" Tell asked. "What other way?"

"Pick somebody else," Newly said. "Somebody you can both face. No, wait, you still die if you lose—"

"Wait," Tell said. "Wait, wait, you've got a good idea here."

"What'd I say?"

"Here's what we do," Tell said. "We pick somebody and make a bet. Whoever kills him wins the money."

"How much money?" Newly asked, interested now.

"Yeah, how much?" Corbett echoed.

"I don't know," Tell said. "We can come up with a figure."

"If it's enough," Newly said, "I'll want in—as long as we ain't facin' each other."

"No," Tell said, "not each other. Somebody else."

"Who?" Corbett asked.

Tell smiled. "That's the part that's gonna make it interestin'."

# TWO

Clint Adams slid his hands beneath the woman's naked buttocks, lifted her up, and pressed her against the wall. She gasped as he pushed deeper into her, wrapping her legs around his waist, taking some of her weight out of his hands. Not that she was heavy. Angela Desmond was only about five feet four and, for the most part, slender, except for an impressive butt. Her breasts were small and round, like ripe peaches, and if anything her weight was pleasant.

"Oh, God," she said as he drove into her, pressing her flat against the wall, the hard surface giving him the maximum penetration that a mattress would not have offered.

They had been in this room at the Blanchard Hotel in Virginia City, Montana, for two days, and had made love on every surface imaginable. This was the first time, however, that he had pinned her against the wall next to the window that overlooked the muddy main street. They had been taking their meals inside, going out only for short walks to stretch their legs, and then it was right back into the room again.

They'd had a discussion the first night they had met,

which had started out as simple, honest flirtation, and had developed into something of a challenge.

A sexual challenge . . .

Angela was a confident woman in her late twenties who had come to Virginia City to run the newspaper, *The Madisonian*. Clint was just passing through, and had gotten into a poker game at the Nugget Saloon. Word got around town that the Gunsmith was playing poker at the Nugget. That was all Angela had to hear. She made her way to the saloon to watch and wait, and Clint noticed her.

When the game broke up, Clint had taken all the money at the table, plus a bag full of small gold nuggets from a miner. To show there were no hard feelings, he asked the other four players to drink with him. He was buying. Three of the players took him up on the offer, but the miner stormed out. Apparently, he'd had to work many hours for that small sack of nuggets, and had no desire to drink with the man who had taken them away from him.

"Don't mind him," Angela said to Clint as the miner— a man named Pearce—stormed out. "He's obviously just a sore loser."

Clint turned away from the other three men to face her. She had long brown hair and pale skin, a nose that tilted up just slightly, and a wide, generous mouth that made him think of the word "luscious." He'd noticed her across the room, but was momentarily stunned at how truly lovely she was up close.

She took immediate advantage of the situation.

"My name is Angela Desmond, editor, writer, and sweeper at *The Madisonian*."

*"The Madisonian?"*

"The local newspaper."

"Oh." Clint knew instantly what she was going to ask. "Listen, Miss Desmond—"

"Angela, please."

"Angela. I can't really—"

"You think I'm going to ask you for an interview, don't you, Mr. Adams?" she asked.

"Well, yes . . ." He felt momentarily embarrassed. Was that not her intention? Was he starting to believe in his own reputation? "And the name's Clint."

"Well, Clint, you're right," she said. "I am going to ask for an interview. Now, I know you've probably been asked many times before. . . ."

"Yes," he said, "many times."

"This would be different," she said. "I promise you."

"How?" he asked. "How would it be different?"

She opened her mouth to say something, then stopped short, made a fist, and said to him, "Gimme a minute."

"Miss Desmond—"

"Angela."

"Angela," he said. "I really don't give interviews. I've had bad experiences with the ones I *have* given—"

"That's because people ask you the wrong questions," she said. "They ask about your reputation. About how and why you came to be called the Gunsmith."

He knew she was thinking fast on her feet, but he liked her for it.

"And you wouldn't?"

"No," she said. "I want to learn about the real you. Clint Adams, not the Gunsmith."

"And what would you ask?"

"Well . . . has anyone ever asked you your favorite food?"

"Well, no . . ."

"What you like to drink?"

"No . . ."

"If you read? And if you do read, what you read?"

"Well . . ."

"And what about women?" she asked.

"What about them?"

"What kinds do you like?"

"Well, right about now," he said, "pretty, brown-haired newspaper reporters are high on my list."

That stopped her. She flushed and looked down, momentarily embarrassed.

"That was sweet," she said, "but see, that's the kind of thing I'd ask. How you talk to and interact with women . . ."

"What about you?" he asked.

"I—what about me?"

"What kind of men do you like?"

"Well, at the moment," she said, "tall, handsome men who apparently don't deserve the reputation they have are high in my list."

"Would you have supper with me?"

The question stopped her.

"Uh, well, it's kind of late, I don't think anyone is serving food right now. . . ."

"I meant tomorrow," he said. "Have supper with me tomorrow."

"I don't know. . . ." she said hesitantly.

"I need somebody to show me where to get a good steak in town."

"Um, well," she said, pushing back a lock of her hair from her forehead, "will I be able to interview you while we eat?"

"We can talk about it."

"Talk about the interview?"

"We can talk about whether or not there should be an interview," he said, then added, "and we can continue flirting."

"Flirting?" she asked, frowning. "Is that what we're doing?"

"Well," he answered, "if we're not, then I'm reading all of the signs wrong."

"And do you usually do that?"

"Do what?"

"Read the signs right?"

"Almost always."

"Well . . ." she said, "then I guess we can talk about that too."

"At supper tomorrow?"

She nodded and said, "At supper tomorrow."

# THREE

At supper the next evening the flirtation continued. In fact, it progressed and became bolder and bolder.

Angela took him to a restaurant called Goldy's. She said the name came from the fact that the owner opened it with gold he took out of a mine.

"He decided he had enough gold to open this place, and he sold the mine to someone else."

"Wasn't that foolhardy?"

"In what way?"

"What if the mine was a bonanza?"

"He didn't care," she said. "He only wanted to make enough to open this place."

Clint looked around. The place was simple, clean, had about ten tables. It did not look like a man's dream come true.

"Wait until you taste the steak," she told him, touching his hand. "You'll see."

And she was right. When the steaks came they were great. As good as any he'd had in restaurants in Denver or San Francisco.

The owner was a man in his fifties named Danny

Flynn, who told Clint that of all the jobs he'd ever had he hated mining the most.

"Even though you were taking gold out of the mine?" Clint asked.

"It didn't matter," Flynn said with an Irish accent. "I hated what I was doing, so I only did it long enough to get me to where I could do what I love to do."

"Cook."

"I'm a natural, laddie," Flynn said. "You've tasted my food. It would be a sin to waste the talent God's seen fit to give me."

"Oh, I agree," Clint said. "I admire the decision you made. I don't know that I could have walked away from the gold."

"Well," Flynn said a bit sheepishly, "I didn't really walk away from all that much gold."

"The mine played out?"

Flynn nodded. "Just a few months after I sold it."

"And the new owners?"

"They took some gold out—probably more than I did—but it was no bonanza, let me tell you. It would not have been worth my time." He spread his arms. "I'm very happy with what I have here."

By the time he finished telling his story, the place—which had been empty when Clint and Angela first arrived—had filled to the point where almost every table was occupied. Clint was starting to think that maybe Danny Flynn had not given up a gold mine after all.

During dessert the subject got down to sex. The flirting was apparently done with. It was time for plain talk, with no games.

"Of course I've had sex," she told him. "But we're not

talking about me. We're talking about your reputation with the ladies."

"I didn't know I had a reputation with the ladies," he said.

"You think all people talk about is how fast the Gunsmith is with a gun?" she asked. "Then you haven't heard your own stories, have you?"

"To tell you the truth, I try not to listen to them," he told her.

"Well, believe me," she said, "that reputation is considerable." She leaned forward, placed her elbows on the table, and lowered her voice. "In fact, that's the one I'm interested in right now."

"Are you telling me that's what you want to interview me about?" he asked.

"Actually," she said, touching the back of his hand, "I was thinking about . . . research."

Clint sat back and stared at her.

"Uh-oh," she said, also sitting back. "Too bold?"

"No," he said, "no, not at all. Unexpectedly bold, I guess, but certainly not too bold."

"Shall we get out of here then?" she asked. "I'm guessing you don't plan to be in town for very long, so I might as well take advantage of this bold streak I'm suddenly showing."

"Actually, you're right," he said. "I was planning on leaving tomorrow."

Clint paid the check, insisting on it since he'd invited her, and they walked out together. They headed for his hotel arm in arm.

"I have a proposition for you," she said.

"What's that?"

"If I can convince you not to leave tomorrow," she said, "you'll give me that interview."

"Angela," he said, "I really am going to leave in the morning."

"Then where's the harm?" she asked. "Let's make it a wager . . . or a challenge."

Clint thought a moment, then said, "Why not?"

# FOUR

And so here it was, two days later, and she had won her sexual challenge. He'd stayed because of her prowess in bed. He didn't know where or how she had learned the things she knew, and didn't care. He was having a hell of a two days, and it was worth an interview.

He grunted as he slammed into her, and she gasped, either from pleasure or from pain, he wasn't sure, but he was too far gone to care. Her face was pressed into his neck, her hard breasts pressing into his chest every time he brought his hips forward. He could feel the heels of her feet in the small of his back, just above his buttocks.

"Oh, God," she moaned into the hollow of his neck. "Yes, harder . . ."

Not pain then . . .

Back in the bed, Clint said, "I was afraid I was going to break your back."

"Haven't you figured out by now I'm not fragile?" she said. "I thought you'd realize that after we broke the dresser."

He looked over at the drawers that were on the floor because the dresser had collapsed beneath their weight.

"So are you still planning to leave tomorrow morning now?" she asked.

"Tomorrow I definitely have to go, Angela."

"I understand," she said.

"Don't even think about giving me another challenge," he warned her.

"I wasn't thinking that," she said. "I think we should go out to supper later, and do my interview, and then finish up here with a night to remember." She slid her hand down over his belly to grasp his semierect penis. "I want to make sure you remember me when you leave here."

As his cock began to swell in her hand, he said, "I don't think there'll be any problem with that."

"Well," she said, rolling toward him and sliding a leg over his thigh, "I just want to make sure."

# FIVE

The three men across the street from the hotel were getting impatient.

"What the hell is he doin' in there?" Bob Lasker asked.

"Didn't ya see him in the window?" the second man, Larry Cameron, said. "He's got him a woman in there who can go for days."

The third man, their boss, said, "We'll just have to wait as long as it takes. You two know your roles, right?"

"We got it," Cameron said. "You only told us four times already."

"I just wanna make sure you got this right," the boss said. "I got a lot ridin' on this."

"So do we," Lasker said. "Yer payin' us a lot of money."

"If we get this done," the boss added.

"Oh," Lasker said, "we'll get 'er done, don't you worry."

"Yeah," Cameron said, "all we need is for him ta come out."

Clint strapped on his gun and said to Angela, "My legs are weak."

"Is that all?" she asked, standing in front of the mirror.

"After being in this room with you for two days, I think my reputation is gone."

"Oh, yeah," he said, "I'm the one who lured you here. Do you care?"

She turned and smiled at him. "Not at all. And after I print my interview, maybe people will realize that I'm somebody to be reckoned with."

"Well," he said, "if I can help that happen, I'm very happy."

She turned, her shirt tucked into her skirt, both of which were the same color as her boots. Her hair was perfect, every strand in place.

"How do I look?" she asked.

"Good enough to eat."

"We better get out of this room while we can," she said. "You can talk to me like that later, when we get back."

He held the door open and said, "After you, ma'am."

"Thank you, sir."

Clint closed the door behind them and followed her down the hall, hoping his legs would get him to the restaurant. He wasn't as young as he used to be.

The moment they stepped out the front door of the hotel, Clint knew something was wrong. He could feel it, and he'd been depending on his instincts for too many years to disregard it.

"Go back inside," he told Angela.

"What? Why—"

"Don't ask any questions," he said, giving her a push. "Just go inside. I'll explain later."

But of course, if he was right, there would be no need to explain. She'd see for herself, and it would be better than any interview.

Once he knew Angela was safely inside the hotel lobby, he stepped down off the boardwalk into the street.

There were two men directly across the street, staring at him. But they were waiting, not approaching him right away. Waiting for what . . . another man to move into position maybe? Like in a window, or on a rooftop? This wouldn't be the first time somebody tried to bushwhack him and make it look like a fair fight. Of course, once the Gunsmith was dead, who would care if he had a bullet in his back?

Clint would care.

The hair on his neck stood up as the two men across the street straightened up, still staring at him and waiting.

This was good. They weren't ready and didn't know what to do.

He crossed the street to them.

"What do we do?" Cameron asked.

"We do what we came here to do."

"What about Lasker?" Cameron asked. "What if he's not in position?"

"Lasker is just insurance, Cameron," the other man said. "We can do this."

"We can?"

"He's only one man."

"Yeah," Cameron said, "with a legend attached."

"Don't think about that part," his boss told him. "Just think about the man."

# SIX

The two men remained on the boardwalk as Clint reached them, still standing in the street.

"You boys looking for me?" Clint asked.

"What would make you think that?" one of them said. The other looked at the first man, which told Clint that he was the one in charge. Also, the second man's eyes kept flicking up toward a rooftop behind Clint. When this was over, Clint would have him to thank for still being alive.

"You've been standing across the street from my hotel all day," Clint said. "From the way you wear your guns, it's plain to me that you make your living with them. Although, you'd think professionals would keep their guns in better condition."

"Our guns work fine," the first man said.

"Well, okay then," Clint said. "Do what you came to do. I'm hungry."

Now both men's eyes went to a rooftop directly behind Clint—probably the hotel itself—and Clint saw the first man give an almost imperceptible nod.

In one motion Clint drew, turned at the waist, and fired one shot. The bullet struck the man on the rooftop square in the chest. He dropped his rifle and then fell. The weapon hit the ground in front of the hotel before he did.

Clint turned back just as the two men were grabbing for their guns. He fired twice, killing them both instantly.

Even though he knew they were dead, he walked to the bodies, plucked their guns from their holsters, and tossed them away. Then he crossed the street and kicked the rifle away from the body of the first man he'd killed. Only when that was done did he eject the spent shells from his gun and replace them with live ammo. He was holstering his own gun when Angela came out of the hotel, followed by several guests and the desk clerk.

"Oh, my God," she said. "That was amazing. You killed three men with three shots, and one of them was on the roof of the hotel."

"You saw it all?" Clint asked.

"Everything."

"Good," Clint said, "because here comes the sheriff. You can help me explain what happened."

Sheriff Ames Edwards regarded both Clint and Angela across his desk.

"I've got three dead men at the undertaker's," he said.

Clint didn't reply. Angela followed his lead.

Edwards was in his fifties, had been a lawman a long time, and knew very well who Clint was. In fact, he'd known as soon as Clint had ridden into town.

"I knew this would happen when you first rode in," Edwards said. "Time for you to leave town, Adams."

"What a coincidence," Clint said. "Just what I had in mind. But there's something I need first."

"What's that?"

"I want to know who those three were."

Edwards opened his top drawer and took out a few items.

"One's unidentified," he said. "According to the contents of their pockets—and their saddlebags—one of the others is named Bob Lasker."

"I don't know him," Clint said. "What about the third one?"

"He had a telegram in his pocket," the lawman said. "I'm assuming it's to him. His name was Newly Yates."

"Yates . . ." Clint said.

"That name sound familiar?"

"Yeah," Clint said, "but from where?"

"He's one of you," the sheriff said.

"One of me?"

"He makes his way with his gun," Edwards said. "He's for hire."

"Wait a minute," Clint said. "He's a bushwhacker. Don't compare him to me. I've never killed a man who wasn't facing me and trying to kill me."

"So you say," Edwards said. "When are you leaving town?"

"First thing in the morning."

"I'd prefer you leave now."

"You want to make that an order?" Clint asked. "And then enforce it?"

The two men stared at each other, and then Edwards said, "First thing in the morning then."

Clint stood up, reached for the telegram on the desk.

"What are you doin'?" Edwards asked as Clint picked it up.

"I killed him," Clint said, folding the telegram and putting it in his shirt pocket. "I figure I'm entitled to it."

He turned and put his hand out to help Angela to her feet. They left the office together.

# SEVEN

Clint and Angela were seated with steaks in front of them before she started asking questions.

"What did those men want?"

"Other than to kill me? I don't know."

"But . . . why?"

"Normally, I'd say it was just someone looking for a reputation," Clint said. "They saw me in town and decided to try me."

"But not this time?"

"No," he said. "Newly Yates hires out. That means there's a good chance someone hired him to kill me."

"And that bothers you more than if it was just someone trying to get a reputation?"

"Yes," he said. "If he was hired, it makes it personal. If that's the case, I'd like to know who hates me enough to hire someone to kill me."

"But, if he's a professional as you say, why was there a man on the roof behind you—and how did you know he was there?"

Clint studied her for a moment, then said, "If you're going to keep asking questions, we're going to call this our interview."

She frowned.

"You can either go over old ground, or cover this particular incident," he said.

"With your insight?"

"With whatever I can offer, yes."

"All right." She produced a pad and pencil. "How did you know the man with the rifle was there? How did you even know there was trouble?"

Clint explained the situation to her as clearly as he could. He'd "felt" that there was trouble, and the two men in the street had given away the presence of the man on the roof.

"They couldn't not look at him," he told her. "That told me he was there, and where he was."

"Wait," she said, "I want to hear more about you feeling there was trouble. That was why you pushed me back into the hotel? Because of some . . . some instinct?"

"That's exactly right," he said. "It's an instinct I've come to trust, and it's never let me down."

She asked a dozen more questions, writing down all the answers, filling page after page until finally she ran out of pencil lead.

"Clint," she said when they were finished talking and eating, "I would love to come back to your hotel with you tonight, but if I'm going to have this story ready by morning—"

"I understand, Angela," he said. "You're a journalist. That comes first."

"I'm afraid it has to."

In truth, he wasn't disappointed. After killing three men, he really wasn't in the mood for sex.

Outside the restaurant, he asked, "Can I walk you home?"

"I'm not going home," she said. "I'm going right to the office to start on this, and that's only a few doors down."

"All right then," he said. "I'll say good-bye now. I will be leaving in the morning, as I told you and the sheriff."

"B-but, what are you going to do? I mean, about these men, about finding out who hired them?"

He didn't want the answers to those questions in the newspaper, so he said, "I don't know. I'll use my time on the trail to figure that out."

She kissed him quickly then and said, "I have to run."

He hugged her and said, "It was a pleasure, Miss Desmond."

"It was definitely that."

She started to walk away, then turned quickly and asked, "Do you want to give me an address so I can send you a copy?"

"Oh," he said, "I think this is a story that will be picked up by other newspapers."

"Do you really think so?"

He nodded. "I'm sure I'll be seeing it."

She smiled happily, then turned and almost ran down the street to her office.

In his room, Clint took out the telegram he'd taken from the sheriff. It was short and said something about Yates being "first," but he'd better hurry up and make his move. The "others" were waiting. It was signed with one name, "Tell."

"Tell," Clint said aloud. It sounded familiar. And with Yates being "first," did that have anything to do with the attempt?

In the morning, before he left town, he'd check with the telegraph office to see where the telegram had come from. That would be his next stop.

# EIGHT

Jerry Corbett put the newspaper down in front of Tell Barlow and sat across from him.

"Newly didn't make it," he said.

"So I see."

"And he cheated." Corbett leaned across the table and touched the paper with his forefinger. "He had two men with him."

"That wasn't cheating to Newly," Tell said. "That was how he did business."

The other man stared at him.

"You didn't know that about him?" Tell asked. "That he was a bushwhacker?"

"No," Corbett said. "I thought he did his job the way we did."

"He did his job the way he had to," Tell said.

"I always knew he wasn't as good as us with a gun," Corbett said, "but bushwhackin' people . . . man, even I don't do that."

"Well, forget about that now," Tell said. "Now that he's out, the bet's between you and me. I want to go next."

"Naw, naw," Corbett said, "we drew straws, remember? I'm next."

"Really?" Tell asked. "Where is Adams gonna be next?"

"You think you're the only one with a brain, Tell," Corbett said. "If he went through Newly's pockets and found your telegram, he's on his way here."

Tell Barlow sat back in his chair. "I'm impressed."

"I'm not a bushwhacker, Tell," Corbett said, "and I ain't as dumb as Newly either."

"I see that."

Corbett stood up.

"Where are you goin'?" Tell asked.

"I'm gonna meet Adams along the way," Corbett said. He pointed his finger at Barlow. "Don't try to take that money out of the bank."

"You know one of us can't take it out unless the other two are dead."

"Yeah," Corbett said, "I also know you're a smooth talker, and one of them tellers is a young girl."

"Don't worry, Jerry," Tell said. "If you win, the money's yours. Just remember, to win, Adams has to be dead."

"Oh, don't worry," Corbett said, "he will be."

# NINE

Clint rode into Cedar City, Utah, still thinking about the telegram in his pocket. Having checked with the telegraph operator in Virginia City, he knew the message had been sent from a town called Selkirk, Arizona. What he didn't know was why the dead man had kept the telegram in his pocket. Was it so Clint would find it? If that was the case, then someone was certainly waiting for him to arrive in Selkirk.

Clint had been expecting attempts at every stop. Cedar City was no different, and Selkirk wouldn't be when he got there.

He liveried his horse and got himself a room at a small hotel off the main street in town. The lobby wasn't very clean, but the room seemed to be well taken care of. He figured the lobby was not the responsibility of a maid, as the room obviously was.

He had taken to staying in small, out-of-the-way hotels as he made his way to Arizona. He had the feeling there was more behind the attempt on his life in Montana than the normal craving for attention and reputation that most men seemed to have.

He found a small café where he had a meal and some

coffee. He was staying away from saloons whenever he could, unless it was the only way to get some food. Over this meal he wondered—as he had since leaving Montana—if Angela's article had been picked up by any other newspapers around the country. He hadn't seen it, but he knew she'd printed it the very next day. Perhaps whoever had sent the dead man his telegram had seen it in another paper? And knew that Newly Yates was dead? And who were these "others" referred to in the telegram by this man named "Tell"?

When he completed his meal, he paid the bill and went back to his hotel. In his room, he once again unfolded the telegram, which was becoming flimsy from all the handling. He also had the feeling from reading it that Newly Yates and his men had not been "hired" to kill him. They'd come at him for some other reason. Not because they'd been hired, and not just because they were seeking a reputation. Something else was going on.

But what?

He read for a while—the Mark Twain book he was carrying with him—then closed the book and turned in early. He wanted to get an early start in the morning.

Harvey Grote was the town drunk. But everybody liked Harvey, and did what they could for him when they could. For instance, the man who owned the café where Clint had eaten often fed Harvey, although he never let him actually enter the café.

Usually, Harvey ate outside, or in the back room. On this night he had been sitting in the back room, eating some scraps, when he saw a man enter the dining room. He choked on his scraps and stared, remaining in the back room until that man left. Only then did Harvey leave the back room by the back door, and run to a house at the south edge of town.

He banged on the door for several minutes before a man answered.

"Harvey, what the hell are you doin'—"

"I gotta talk to ya, Sheriff," Harvey said. "It's real important."

"Are you drunk?"

"Sheriff," the man said, "I'm always drunk, you know that, but I ain't so drunk that I don't know I saw what I just saw."

"Harvey, I'm havin' dinner with my wife."

"I know, Sheriff," Harvey said, "I figgered, but this is real important."

"Is that Harvey Grote?" a woman's voice called.

"Yes, Miriam," Sheriff Andrew Taylor said. "I'll get rid of him—"

"Let him in," Miriam Taylor said. "I'll fix him a plate."

Sheriff Taylor said to Harvey, "You're lucky I'm married to a saint," and let him in.

"Okay, Harvey," Sheriff Taylor said, "how do you know this?"

"I was there, Sheriff," Harvey said around the chicken and dumplings that were in his mouth. This was a hell of a lot better than the scraps he got from the café. "I saw him come in, and I saw him go out."

"No, Harve," Taylor said. "I mean, how do you know it was him?"

"I saw him kill three men in Abilene."

"He's a killer?" Miriam asked.

They was tryin' ta kill *him,* ma'am," Harvey said. "He give them every chance to walk away, but they wouldn't."

"I see." She looked at her husband. "This sounds like the kind of man you need, Andrew."

"He's obviously just passin' through," Taylor said. "Why would he decide to stay?"

"Because you're the law, sweetheart," Miriam said. "You could make him stay."

"We can talk about this later, dear," he said, nodding his head toward Harvey.

The town drunk finished his food and thanked Miriam effusively for it. He was then walked to the door and shown out, thanked by the sheriff for his information.

"You have to do something," Miriam said as Taylor returned to the kitchen.

"Even if Harvey is right," Taylor said, "there's no way I can stop Adams from leavin' if he wants."

"Yes, there is," Miriam said.

"Like what?"

"Like arresting him."

"And what good would it do to put him in a cell?"

"Then talk to him," she said. "Ask him for help."

"Why would he—"

"Why wouldn't he?" she asked. "You won't know until you ask him."

"All right," he said, "tomorrow morning."

"Tomorrow he may be gone," she said. "Tonight."

"Tonight?"

She nodded. "Now."

"Now?"

She nodded.

He sighed, strapped on his gun, kissed his wife, and left the house.

# TEN

The halfhearted knock on Clint's door woke him. Not that he was sleeping that soundly. It was too early for him to turn in, and his body was telling him that.

He went to the door after pulling on his trousers, holding his gun in his right hand behind his back. He was surprised when he saw the badge on the man standing in the hall.

"Are you Clint Adams?"

"What did I do?" he asked. "I just got to town a few hours ago."

"You didn't do nothin', Mr. Adams. I'm Sheriff Andrew Taylor. Can I come in and talk to you for a minute?"

"I haven't done anything?"

"Not that I know of."

"All right," Clint said. "Come in."

He walked away from the door, slid his gun back into the holster that was hanging on the bedpost, then turned to face the lawman, who had come in and closed the door behind him.

"I really don't know how to start," the lawman said. Abruptly, he removed his hat and held it in front of him.

"Why not start at the beginning?" Clint asked.

35

"Actually," Taylor said, "that's too far back. I might as well just be frank with you."

"That would be refreshing."

"I need your help," Taylor said, "and by that I mean, I need your gun. In three days' time a gang is coming to town, led by Ned Pine. Do you know that name?"

"Afraid I don't."

"Well, you probably wouldn't. Ned's tryin' to make a name for himself. So far he's only known locally."

"So what's he going to do?" Clint asked. "Take the town over? Level it?"

"Well," Taylor said, "the message he sent me said that if I was still here when him and his boys arrived, they were gonna kill me. See, he's givin' me a chance to run."

"How many men has he got riding with him?"

"Close to a dozen."

"And how many deputies do you have?"

"I had two," Taylor said, "but they resigned when they heard what Pine is plannin'."

"And you haven't been able to hire any new ones?" Clint asked.

"No."

"Nobody in town will help you?"

"That's right."

Clint shrugged. "I'd say take the chance he's giving you and run."

"That's what my wife says."

"Sounds like a smart woman," Clint said. "I'd listen to her."

"That would be the smart thing to do," Sheriff Taylor admitted.

"You'd still be alive, and your wife would still have a husband," Clint said. "Any kids?"

"None. We've been married about five years, no kids yet."

"Do you want kids?"

"Yeah," he said, "we both want 'em."

"Well, you've got to be alive to have kids."

"I know that." He was rotating his hat in his hands. "I told my wife. . . ."

"Told her what?"

"She's the one told me to come and talk to you," Taylor said. "I told her you have no reason to help me."

"You're right."

"Yeah, I know."

"So you don't intend to leave, do you?"

"I can't," Taylor said. "I take my job very seriously. I plan to wear a badge for a long time. I'd never get a job anywhere else if word got around that I ran."

"You any good with that gun?"

"Fair."

"You still got three days to find some help."

"I know it," the lawman said. "I've been sending telegrams. I got a brother might show up in time. He's in California. Might not show up."

"He any good with a gun?"

"He's a gambler," Taylor said. "A bad one, and he's worse with a gun."

"Doesn't sound like he'd be much help."

"Probably not," Taylor said. "My stubbornness would probably get him killed as well as myself."

"Still sounds like you should run," Clint said. "Doesn't sound like the town is going to back you, so why should you risk your life for them?"

"Ain't for them," Taylor said, putting on his hat. "It's for this."

He tapped his badge with a fingernail.

"I wore a badge for a while, when I was younger," Clint said. "It was situations like this that made me take it off for good."

"I don't blame you." Taylor reached for the doorknob. "Well, thanks for listening. Enjoy the town, but if I was you I'd be gone in two days. Just a warning."

"Thanks," Clint said. "I'm just passing through, so that shouldn't be a problem."

Taylor nodded, went out the door.

Clint was awake now. He walked to the window, which overlooked the front of the hotel, and watched the lawman leave and walk away up the street. Over the years he'd known a lot of lawmen like Andrew Taylor. Too stubborn to do the right thing, because the right thing would be seen as the cowardly thing.

Clint had known a good man with a gun to hold off a mob. But a gang with guns, that was a tough one. He didn't know any single man—not Wyatt Earp, not Bat Masterson, not Hickok—who could face twelve men alone.

He felt sorry for Taylor, and sorrier for his wife, but there wasn't any reason for him to take a hand in the sheriff's problem. On top of not knowing the man, he'd never known two men to stand off a dozen and live through it.

He'd be as big a fool as Sheriff Taylor if he decided to try.

# ELEVEN

Clint was dressing the next morning when there was another knock on his door—more forceful than the sheriff's knock the night before. He doubted it was the lawman. He'd made himself perfectly clear the night before. He strapped on his gun and walked to the door. When he opened it, he found an attractive brunette in her early thirties standing there, glaring at him. She was wearing a gingham dress with a high neck. He doubted it was deliberate, but the cut of the dress showed off her full bosom.

"Mrs. Taylor?"

She looked shocked. "How did you know?"

"From what your husband told me last night," he replied, "I should have expected you. Do you mind if we talk over breakfast?"

"I have had my breakfast, Mr. Adams."

"Well, I haven't." He stepped out into the hall, forcing her to step back, and closed the door behind him. "If you want to talk to me, you're going to have to take me someplace to eat."

"Well . . . very well. There's a small café not far from here that's pretty good."

Fine," he said. "Lead the way."

• • •

The café was half full, and the people who were there gave the sheriff's wife odd looks as she entered and sat with a strange man.

"I'm sorry," Clint said. "I guess I'm ruining your reputation."

"Don't worry about my reputation, sir," she said. "I'm more concerned with my husband's life, and these good people don't give a fig about that."

"Mrs. Taylor," Clint said, "did your husband tell you what I advised him last night?"

"Yes, he did," she said. "You gave him the same advice I did. He's not going to take it from either of us. Besides, he did not come to you for advice."

"Well," Clint said, "that was all I had to give him, I'm afraid."

"No," Miriam Taylor said, "you had a lot more to offer him."

Clint was about to answer when a waiter appeared. Quickly, Clint said, "Steak, eggs, and coffee."

When he was gone, Clint asked, "What are you talking about, Mrs. Taylor?"

"Your gun," she said. "You hire your gun out, don't you?"

"No, I don't."

That stopped her for a moment. She sat back and stared at him.

"What do you mean, no?" she asked. "You're a gunfighter, aren't you? By the very definition you hire your gun ou—"

"Mrs. Taylor—what's your first name?"

"Wha—it's Miriam. But why do you—"

"Miriam," he said, "since we're getting intimate here, I figure I'm entitled to call you by your first name."

"Wha—I—how dare you? We're not getting intimate," she stammered.

"We are if you're calling me a gunfighter," he said. "See, that means I have to correct you and tell you what I actually am."

"I don't—are you claiming that you are not a gun-fighter?"

"I'm not claiming anything, Miriam," he said. "I'm telling you I'm not a gunfighter."

"But—then what are you?"

"See?" he said. "You're getting intimate."

She sat back in her chair again and stared at him.

"I think I know what you are, Mr. Adams."

"And what's that. Miriam?"

She leaned forward and said, "Impossible!"


Miriam Taylor did not storm off, as Clint thought she might. She was still there when the waiter brought his breakfast. He had to admire her not only for her loyalty to her husband, but for her beauty.

"Well?" she asked, her arms folded beneath her full breasts.

"What? I'm sorry, did you ask me something?"

"You said you were going to tell me what you are," she said. "I'm waiting."

"I'm just a man, Miriam," he said. "That's all."

"But . . . you do have a reputation with a gun."

"Yes."

"And you are very good with it, aren't you?"

"Yes, I am," he said. "I'm a man who is very good with a gun."

"Very well then," she said, looking satisfied. "We're back to where we started, aren't we?"

Around a mouthful of eggs he asked, "And where is that?"

"Why won't you help my husband?"

# TWELVE

"Miriam," Clint said, "I don't know your husband, I don't know this town. I'm just passing through. I—I don't have any reason to risk my life to help him."

"He's the law."

"I appreciate that."

"No one here will help him."

"I realize—"

"He'll be killed!" She gripped the edges of the table tightly.

"I'm sorry about that," Clint said. "He won't be killed if he takes you and leaves town. Why doesn't he think of you?"

"That's between me and my husband," she said. "He's an honorable man. He accepted that badge and agreed to do a job."

"His job is not getting killed for no reason," Clint said. "If the town won't help him, why should he help the town?"

"This man—this outlaw—Pine, whatever his name is—" she stammered.

"Ned Pine."

"Yes. He has not threatened the town in any way, only my husband."

"Why?"

"Because Andrew was doing his job one night, and put Pine and one of his men in a cell to sleep off a drunk. Pine took offense, said Andrew would never have been able to do that if he hadn't been drunk."

"So for that he threatens to come back with twelve men and kill your husband?"

"I don't know how many men he has, or how many he will bring with him," she said. "He told Andrew he would come back in one week's time, face him in the street, and gun him down."

That wasn't the story the sheriff had told Clint.

"Miriam, how good is your husband with a gun?"

"He can handle a gun," she said, "but he's no gunman. He is not a . . . a fast-draw artist."

"And Pine?"

"I don't know anything about the man," she said. "Andrew won't talk to me about him."

Clint was finished with his breakfast and pushed the plate away, the food only half-eaten. Miriam Taylor had done her best to ruin his appetite, and had succeeded.

"I'm not promising anything," he told her, "but I'm going to ask some questions."

"What kind of questions?" she asked. "Ask them of who?"

"I'm going to find out what kind of man Ned Pine is," he said, "and I'll ask people in town who I think might know."

"Like who?"

"Well, I'll start with the newspaper editor."

"Paul Deering," she said. "He'll talk to you."

"Good," Clint said. "That shouldn't take me very long."

"So you still plan to leave town today?"

"That's my plan," he said, "yes."

"Then what good will asking questions do?" she demanded.

"I don't know, Miriam," he said. "All I know is I'm going to ask, and see what happens from there."

"So all I've managed to do is delay your departure?" she asked.

"So far, yes."

She sat back. "Well, at least I've accomplished that."

Yes, and he wasn't at all sure how she'd done it.

They left the café together and she pointed down the street.

"The newspaper office is two blocks that way," she said. "Tell Paul I sent you to see him. He'll talk freely to you."

"All right."

"I don't know who else you will be talking to," she said, "but I truly hope you'll hear something that will make you reconsider helping my husband."

"I am trying to help your husband, Miriam."

"No," she said. "I mean, by standing with him."

"By using my gun?"

"Yes."

Clint didn't understand why Taylor would need his gun if Pine wanted to meet him in the street for a fair fight. If that was the case, then Andrew Taylor only had to do his job, or take off the badge.

"I hope I see you again, Mr. Adams."

"If you do," he told her, "you better call me Clint."

# THIRTEEN

When Clint reached the office of the *Cedar City Gazette,*
he found the door unlocked. There were some past issues
taped in the windows, which he found odd. They were
yellow with age, and some were difficult to read. He wondered if they were just being used as cheap shades to keep
the sun out.

He entered, and the place was quiet. The office was set
up like most newspaper offices. He was in the room with
the press, and there was a man in another room seated at
a desk. Clint walked to the open doorway and knocked.
The man looked up, pushed a pair of wire-framed specta-
cles up onto his head so he could see, then waved.

Clint entered and the man said, "Help ya?"

"Are you Paul Deering?"

"That's me."

Clint thought the man was eighty if he was a day, and
he was painfully thin.

"The sheriff's wife, Miriam, sent me over to talk to
you."

"That woman is a saint," Deering said. "And who might
you be?"

"My name's Clint Adams."

Now the man peered at Clint's face intently. "Yer tellin' me yer the Gunsmith?"

"That's right."

"And Miriam sent ya to me?"

"Yes."

"For what? An interview?"

"No." Clint had already had his fill of interviews. "I need to ask some questions about Ned Pine."

"That dirty lowlife?" Deering asked. "Why are you interested in him?"

"It's complicated," Clint said. "It appears he's promised to kill the sheriff in two days' time."

"That's right," Deering said. "Said a week ago he'd be back to do it. So? Oh, I get it. Miriam wants you to kill Pine."

"I guess you could say that."

"Well, I gotta tell ya, you'd be exterminatin' a varmint, not killin' a man."

"What I don't understand is why I should do it," Clint said. "I only came to town yesterday. I'm just passing through, and already both the sheriff and his wife have come to me for help."

"Andy Taylor came to you?"

"Last night, in my room."

"Ah," Deering said, waving a hand, "that's only 'cause Miriam made him do it."

"Yeah, he told me that too. He also told me his deputies quit on him and nobody in town wants the job."

"Town's full of cowards," Deering said. "If I was ten years younger, I'd grab a rifle and back him myself."

"Tell me, Mr. Deering," Clint said, "how good is the sheriff with a gun?"

Deering studied Clint for a few moments, then said, "Look, when you came in I told you Miriam Taylor was a saint. That's true as far as it goes."

"What do you mean?"

"What she's also done is ruin a perfectly good lawman."

"Now I'm not following."

"Andy Taylor has been sheriff of this town for four-teen years. For nine of those years he was a damned good one. He handled everything that came along, and he wasn't afraid to face down men with guns."

"And now?"

"Well, since he got married about five years ago, he's just not the same man."

"And that's because he got married?" Clint asked. "Or because he married Miriam?"

Deering hesitated, then said, "A little bit of both, I guess."

"So does she want him to give up his badge?"

"Oh, yeah, been after him for years to do it—and pretty soon he'll give in."

"Seems to me now would be the time," Clint said. "What can you tell me about Ned Pine?"

"Fast with a gun," Deering said, "and deadly accurate."

"I've never heard of him."

"Local boy," Deering said, "can't be more than twenty-five. The sheriff has known him since he was about eleven."

"So why does Pine want to kill him?"

"Because he's been bad since he could walk, that one," the newspaper editor said.

"Where's his family?"

"Ridin' with him," Deering said. "A buncha cousins. They're a bad bunch—but he's the worst of 'em."

"So tell me," Clint asked, "if the sheriff steps into the street with Ned Pine . . ."

"He's as good as dead."

# FOURTEEN

"You did what?"

Sheriff Andy Taylor stared at his wife across his desk in the jailhouse.

"I went to see Mr. Adams," Miriam said.

"What did you do that for?"

"I wanted to ask him to help you," she said. "I wanted to know why he would not."

"My God," Taylor said, putting his head in his hands, "what does he think of me now, having my wife go to him to ask for help?"

"You didn't send me," she said. "I went on my own."

"The fact of the matter is you went," he said. "It doesn't matter who sent you."

"What's wrong with that?"

Taylor raised his head to look at his wife.

"Miriam, a man doesn't let his wife fight his battles for him."

"I'm doing no such thing," she said. "I'm just trying to help."

"Well, do me a favor," he said. "Don't try to help anymore."

"What kind of way is that to talk?" she demanded.

51

"You won't take off that silly badge so we can go live in a civilized place, and now you expect me to just sit back and watch you get killed—leaving me here, where I never wanted to be."

"Miriam—"

"You're a selfish man, Andy Taylor," she said, heading for the door. "That's all I have to say."

But it wasn't. As she got to the door, she turned and added, "And I'll tell you another thing. He looked at me like I was a woman, which is more than I can say for you lately."

"What the—" he began, but she was out the door and gone.

Clint Adams left the newspaper office with the name of another person Deering said he should talk to. It was Charles Wentworth, the former mayor of Cedar City. Deering said that Wentworth knew all there was to know about Ned Pine. Clint didn't know why, but he intended to ask him. . . .

"The boy is my nephew."

The former mayor was only too happy to talk about Ned Pine—or anything else, for that matter. Clint found him sitting on the porch alone, and had the feeling from the welcome he got that the man sat there a lot. He seemed almost as old as the newspaper editor.

"I was mayor of this town for twelve years, but I've been out of office now for ten. I knew that boy as bad even in the cradle."

"I understand he has cousins riding with him," Clint said.

"None of mine," Wentworth said. "I was a politician, Mr. Adams. I had no time for foolishness like raising kids. And when I see how my brother's offspring turned out, I know I made the right decision."

Wentworth's house was a two-story brick affair in what was obviously the more affluent part of town. When he offered Clint a drink, a black man wearing white gloves brought out a bottle of bourbon and two glasses on a tray and set it down on a table at the former mayor's elbow. Wentworth may have been an ex-mayor, but he still dressed the part, wearing a three-piece suit and a watch fob.

"We'll pour, Cyrus."

"Yassuh," the servant said, and withdrew.

"Would you mind?" Wentworth asked Clint. "My hands aren't as steady as they once were."

"Of course."

Clint poured two glasses and handed Wentworth one of them.

"Don't want Cyrus waitin' on me hand and foot, although he probably will before long."

The man took a sip and closed his eyes as it worked its way down.

"Excellent."

Clint sipped the bourbon and nodded his appreciation. He knew good whiskey, even though he preferred a cold beer.

"What can I tell you, Mr. Adams?"

"Well . . . your nephew has threatened to kill the sheriff."

"The man's as good as dead," Wentworth said with a wave of his hand.

"Really? You're that sure?"

"Bad seed, Mr. Adams," Wentworth said. "The boy is a bad seed. He'd kill you as soon as look at you."

"I see."

"If he says he's going to kill Andy Taylor, then he'll do it."

"What about the rest of them?"

"He's got several cousins with him, and the rest are just trash."

"What will they do to the town if there's no lawman?" Clint asked.

"What trash does," Wentworth said.

"Why not bring in federal help then?"

"Not up to me," Wentworth said. "I ain't the mayor anymore. You better ask the present mayor—or better yet, ask the sheriff himself."

"I think I'll do that, Mr. Wentworth."

He finished his bourbon and set the empty glass down on the table.

"Pour me another before you go, will you, son?" the old man asked.

"Sure," Clint said, and obliged.

As he was going down the steps from the porch, he turned and asked, "How did Ned become Ned Pine?"

Wentworth laughed.

"Who would be frightened of an outlaw named Ned Wentworth?"

The man had a point.

# FIFTEEN

Clint knew he should just saddle Eclipse, mount up, and ride out of town. He knew this even as he was walking to the sheriff's office. When he entered, the man looked up from his desk and did not look happy to see him.

"What do you want?"

Clint was taken aback by the man's attitude. Wasn't this the same lawman who just last night had been asking him for help?

"Your wife came to see me this morning."

"So I heard," Taylor said. "Just so you know, I didn't send her."

"I know that," Clint said. "She told me she came on her own. She seems to be an extraordinary woman."

"Really? What else do you think about her? Is she beautiful?"

"You're married to her," Clint said. "You know the answer to that is yes."

"And did you tell her that?"

Clint was puzzled. "No, I didn't. We didn't talk about her looks, Sheriff. We talked about you."

"Yeah, well . . ."

"What's on your mind?"

"She told me you looked at her like she was a woman," Taylor complained.

"Don't you look at her that way?"

"Well . . . I thought I did."

"Oh, I get it," Clint said. "Your wife is feeling unappreciated, is that it?"

"I suppose so."

"And she blames your job?" Clint asked. "And the badge?"

"Actually, yes."

"Sheriff," Clint said, "it sounds like you need to work on your marriage, but to do that you have to stay alive."

"Sounds like you're gonna tell me again to run."

"As far and as fast as you can."

"I can't do that."

"Believe me, I understand," Clint said. "Can I sit down?"

"Sure. You want some coffee?" He pointed. "Pot's on the stove, cup hanging on the wall."

"Thanks."

Clint walked to the potbelly stove, took a tin cup from a hook on the wall, and poured himself some coffee from the cast-iron pot. He took the cup with him and sat opposite the sheriff.

"As I understand it," Clint said, "Ned Pine wants to face you in the street alone, you and him. That's not what you told me."

"Who told you that? Miriam?"

"I've talked to a few people in town," Clint said.

"Well, what Ned Pine says he's gonna do and what he does are two different things. He may want to face me in the street, and that's fine, but his boys will all be there. If I should outdraw him and kill him, I know they'd gun me down in the street."

Clint shook his head and put his cup down on the desk in front of him, then moved to the edge of his seat.

"See, this is what I don't get," he said. "I understand about being a man, and about doing what's right and what's expected of you. I also understand having a responsibility to something. What I don't understand is why you'd step out onto the street knowing you were going to be killed."

"Look," Taylor said. "I don't have your reputation," he said. "Maybe you can walk away from a fight, but I can't. If I do that, I'll never wear a badge again."

Clint sat back. This wasn't his fight, so why was he even still in town, talking to this man, talking to Deering and Wentworth?

Well, the answer to that was simple—Miriam Taylor. An extraordinary woman, yes, and a beauty. And another man's wife. Clint didn't make a habit of pursuing married women. If he stayed in Cedar City, there was all kinds of trouble on the horizon—not the least of which was twelve or more men with guns.

"Look," the lawman said, "never mind what my wife told you. This ain't your fight."

Clint was surprised. It was as if the man was reading his mind. "I know it's not," Clint said. "The problem is I now know that you're going to step into the street and, one way or another, you're going to end up dead."

"Probably."

Clint shook his head. "I can't just ride out of town knowing you're going to do that."

"So what does that mean?" Taylor asked.

"It means I'll offer you my help," Clint said, "if you still want it."

# SIXTEEN

Clint refused to wear a deputy's badge.

"I'm not taking a job, Sheriff," he said. "I'm just a civilian offering my help."

"Okay." Taylor put the badge back in his desk's top drawer.

"And let's get something else straight," Clint added, "or we're not going to be able to work together."

"What's that?"

"I'm not after your wife," Clint said. "I don't make a habit of going after married women. And I'm not looking for a wife of my own. I don't need a woman. . . ."

"Go ahead, say it," Taylor said. "You don't need a woman who doesn't know her place."

"That's not exactly what I was going to say," Clint said.

"Look, I'm embarrassed by the fact that she came to see you. If I'd known she was gonna do that—"

"It's done, and it's over," Clint said. "Now we need to concentrate on Ned Pine and his men. We can't just assume that he's bringing a dozen men with him. We need to know how many, and who they are. Can we get that information?"

"I've been working on that myself," Taylor said. "Pine's got one cousin who's still in town. I was gonna go question him."

"Good, we can do that together."

"And you'll come to the house for supper tonight," Taylor said.

"Do you think that's wise?"

"Miriam would insist, just to be a good hostess. Don't worry, she's not gonna be part of this. As far as I'm concerned she's played her part already."

And played it well, Clint thought. But he was going to be glad if he didn't have to deal with the strong-willed woman again beyond supper.

"I hear you've been a lawman for a long time, and I don't want to step on your toes, but—"

"Hey," Taylor said, "I know your reputation, Adams. Just tell me what you want to do."

"First, I'd like to check out your gun."

"My gun?"

"And your office guns—rifles, shotguns, whatever you've got."

"No problem," Taylor said.

He unlocked the gun rack on the wall so Clint could check the Winchesters and shotguns there. They all seemed to be clean, and in proper working order.

"You got guns at home?" Clint asked.

"Just like the office," Taylor said. "Rifle and shotgun."

"I'll check on them tonight. Let me see your Colt." Clint held out his hand. Taylor removed his gun from his holster and handed it over. Clint quickly unloaded it, broke it down on the desktop, examined it, and then reassembled it.

"I've never seen anybody do that so fast," Taylor said.

Clint handed the gun back. "You seem to take care of your weapons."

"Like you said," Taylor replied, "I've been a lawman for a long time."

"And you've never come up against a situation like this before?"

"Oh, sure," Taylor said, "but I had deputies, and no wife. That, uh, seemed to make a difference."

"You know," Clint said, "I have to tell you a married lawman is something I can't really understand. When you've got somebody waiting for you at home, I don't think you can do the job the way it needs to be done."

"You might be right," Taylor said. "After this, I guess I'll have some thinking to do."

Clint wondered if he meant thinking about whether or not he still wanted to be a lawman, or a husband.

# SEVENTEEN

The Taylor house was warm and filled with aromatic smells coming from the kitchen. Whatever else Miriam Taylor was, she was apparently a good cook.

Clint and Andy Taylor were in the living room holding glasses of whiskey.

"It's all I have in the house," Taylor had said, and Clint told him it was fine. When Miriam joined them, she also held a glass of whiskey, which she sipped without a hint of daintiness.

"I'm so happy you came around to our way of thinking, Clint," she said.

"Miriam," Taylor said, "Clint has decided to help us because—"

"I talked him into it," she said, interrupting her husband. "Isn't that right, Clint?"

Clint just lifted his glass to her and said, "That's exactly right, Miriam."

At the dinner table, she asked, "So what are we going to do about Ned Pine? Arrest him as soon as he shows his face? Go out and hunt him down?"

"Miriam . . ." Taylor said warningly.

"Am I not to ask?" she said. "Not to be curious?"

"It really wouldn't be smart for two men to hunt down a dozen or more, Miriam," Clint said.

"No smarter for a man to meet them in the street."

"Pine wants to meet me man-to-man, Miriam," Taylor said.

"Well, even you said he'll have his men backing him up," she pointed out. "Will it be enough to have the Gunsmith backing *you* up?"

"Probably not," Clint said.

"Well, what if we somehow passed the word that Clint Adams was a deputy—"

"I'm not a deputy," Clint said.

"I beg your pardon?"

"Clint is not wearing a badge."

"Why—"

"It's his choice, Miriam," Taylor said, cutting her off. "He's offered his help. Let's not question him about it."

"Very well," she said. "I'm just the wife, I'm not to ask any questions."

Clint did not respond. It was up to Taylor to deal with his wife's feelings.

But Taylor avoided that problem for the rest of the meal, and eventually Clint found himself on the front porch with the sheriff, each with an after-dinner cigar.

"You said you were just passin' through when you got here," Taylor commented.

"That's right."

"What are we keeping you from?" the lawman asked. "Where were you headed?"

Clint decided to tell Taylor the truth. There was no harm. He explained how someone had tried to kill him under strange circumstances and he was on his way to try to find out why.

"He had a telegram in his pocket?" Taylor asked.

"That's right."

"And you're going to the town the telegram originated from?"

"Right again."

"And you don't think that might be a trap?"

"I'm sure it is," Clint said.

"And you're still goin'?"

"That's where my answers are."

Taylor had been staring straight out at the lights of the town, but now he turned to face Clint.

"So how is that different from what you're accusing me of doin'?"

"Well," Clint said, "first of all, I don't have a wife to think of, or a job. I'm on my own."

"And second of all," Taylor said helpfully, "you're the Gunsmith."

"I was going to say, second of all, I'm not you," Clint replied, "but that amounts to the same thing, I guess."

"So what will you do if you get where you're goin' and there are twelve guns waitin' for you?"

"If that happens I'll have three options," Clint said.

"What are they?"

"Turn around and leave, forget about it."

"And second?"

"Find help."

"I can't see you walkin' away," Taylor said, "so my guess is you'd look for help. Somebody like Wyatt Earp or Bat Masterson?"

"Or both," Clint said, "or some other friend. But don't be so sure I wouldn't walk away. If I couldn't find any help, I'd be down to my third option."

"And what would that be?"

Clint let out a cloud of blue smoke and said into it, "Die."

# EIGHTEEN

When the knock came at Clint's door later that night, he frowned. He put down the Twain book and grabbed his gun. Now what? Or more precisely, who? Maybe Taylor had thought of something else he wanted to talk about.

He opened the door as he had the night before, with the gun behind his back. He was surprised to see Miriam Taylor, not the sheriff. She had a shawl pulled tightly around her.

"Miriam, what are you doing here?"

"I wanted to talk to you without Andy around," she said. "May I come in, or must we do it out here in the hall?"

"Yes, all right. Come in."

She entered and watched him holster the gun.

"It must be a terrible way to live," she said, "to have to answer every knock on your door with a gun in your hand."

"It becomes second nature," he said. "What's on your mind? Did I not thank you enough for the delicious dinner?"

"Well, you're testy."

"You're another man's wife in my room late at night, Miriam," he said. "That's not a comfortable position for me to be in."

She laughed briefly. He was aware of her smell, as if she'd just stepped from a bath.

"Don't tell me you're afraid of Andy."

"If anything," he said, "I'm more afraid of you. Does he know you came here to see me?"

"Oh, no. He'd never stand for that."

"Where does he think you are?"

"Visiting a sick friend."

"That's a very old excuse," he said. "Did he believe you?"

"Yes," she said, "because I do have a sick friend in town, a dear lady who has pneumonia. I've been looking in on her for the doctor, who's been very busy lately."

"Then what are you doing here?" he asked. "You should be with her."

"I checked on her on the way here," Miriam said. "She's just fine, sleeping like a baby."

"What made you think I wouldn't be sleeping like a baby?"

"A man like you? You wouldn't be asleep this early. I am wondering, however, why you're not at one of our fine saloons, making the acquaintance of our fine saloon girls and whores."

"Actually, I was trying to keep a low profile, but I guess there's not much point in that while I'm dealing with you and your husband."

"I'm sorry it's such a hardship."

"It's going to be a hardship, Miriam," Clint said. "It's going to be a hell of a hardship when Ned Pine arrives."

"Well, I just wanted to come over and thank you personally for agreeing to help Andy."

"You did that," he said. "You thanked me at your house."

"No," she said, "I mean . . . thank you . . . personally."

Abruptly, she let her shawl fall to the floor. It was such

a dramatic move that he expected her to be naked beneath it, but she would never have been able to get out of the house that way.

The fact that she wasn't naked, though, didn't make the situation any less explosive. She was extremely sexual, and he was feeling the effects of it as she undid the buttons of her dress.

"Miriam, don't—"

"Come on, Clint," she said. "I see the way you look at me."

"You're a beautiful woman," he said. "I look at beautiful women."

"Perhaps," she said, "but you want me."

"No," he said, "I don't."

The buttons were undone, and she tugged the top of the dress down so that her shoulders and the upper slopes of her pale breasts were showing. If he allowed her to get to her nipples, he wasn't sure he would be able to resist her. So he took quick steps forward, which she misinterpreted. When he grabbed the edges of her dress and tugged it back up, covering her breasts and shoulders, it surprised her.

"Wha—" she said.

"I told you, don't do it."

"I don't understand."

"I told your husband I wasn't interested in you," he said. "You're another man's wife."

"But you are interested in me."

"But you're another man's wife," he said again. "I draw the line there."

She frowned at him. "Are you serious?"

"Dead serious," he said. "Besides, I don't understand what you think you're doing. I had the impression you loved your husband."

"I did once." She started buttoning her dress.

"When did it change?"

"When I realized he wasn't going to leave this godforsaken town and take me away."

"You thought he would?"

"I thought I could make him eventually."

Clint laughed.

"Don't make fun of me."

"I'm not" he said. "You're just not the first woman to underestimate the lure of the badge."

"Obviously," she said. "You men and your pieces of tin."

"Not me," he said. "I took it off a long time ago, and it stays off."

"Andy Taylor is not the man I thought he was," she said. "That's why I'm here. But I guess you're not the man I thought you were."

"I'm real sorry we both disappointed you, Miriam."

"Yes," she said with a sniff. "So am I."

She left the room without saying good night, leaving her scent in the air. Clint didn't think he could stand it, so he decided to leave until the smell—of woman and sex and soap—dissipated.

He strapped on his gun and headed for the nearest saloon.

# NINETEEN

Miriam Taylor had been right about one thing. He'd wanted her. How could you be in a room with a woman like that with her naked to the waist, and not want her?

So when he found Buckskin Bill's Saloon and entered, he was not only receptive to all the girls working the floor, but they flocked to him. It was as if they could sense that he was ready.

He stood at the bar, drank beer, and flirted with the four girls while trying to decide which one he was going to take back to his room with him.

There was a brunette named Rio, who had big breasts, a Spanish accent, and a bawdy laugh.

A blonde named Santana who was long and leggy and had great big blue eyes.

A redhead—oddly named Raven—with green eyes and a quick smile.

And finally, another brunette named Cory, this one short and nicely chubby.

Clint was leaning toward Rio. He liked her accent and her body, and she was the tallest of the four, which appealed to him tonight.

But Cory, the small brunette, kept rubbing herself

against him, all bulbous breasts and padded hips, and he could feel the heat of her through both of their clothes.

At one point, when all four women were busy working the room, he turned to the bartender and said, "Another beer."

"Comin' up."

He went off, came back with a frothy mug. He put it down on the bar and remained standing there.

"Can I help you?" Clint asked, picking up the mug.

"Want some advice?"

"That depends," Clint said. "About what?"

The man leaned on the bar with his elbows. He was medium height, middle-aged, seemed to know his job well, so Clint thought that whatever bartenderly advice he had—about whatever—might be good.

"Seems to me one of them gals is goin' back to your room with you tonight."

"I was thinking that."

"Well, was I you, I'd forget about Rio."

"Oh? Why's that?"

"She's got a man."

"That's so?"

"Well . . . he sorta thinks she's his girl."

"And what does Rio think?"

"She thinks he's annoyin'."

"Then why should I take him into account?" Clint asked.

"He's big, mean, ugly, and can use a gun."

"Anything else?"

"Yeah," the bartender said. "He's been glaring at you from a corner of the room all night."

"Which corner?"

"Back right."

Clint turned with his beer, looked around the room before zeroing in on that corner. Sure enough, there was a man there who matched the bartender's description. He was glowering at that moment, more than glaring.

"What's your name?" Clint asked the bartender.

"Bruno."

"Bruno, what's that fella's name?"

"His name is Winston," Bruno said.

"Winston?"

"Yeah," Bruno said, "it's part of what makes him so mean."

"And what does he do for a living?"

"Works on one of the ranches," Bruno said. "I understand he pulls tree trunks out of the ground—with his hands."

"And he can use a gun?"

"Yep."

"How good?"

"He hits what he aims at."

"Come on, Bruno," Clint said. "I want to know if he's killed anybody."

"Lately?"

Clint reached out and grabbed Bruno by the shirt. He was short-tempered because he'd had to turn Miriam Taylor away, and because he was still in town when he was supposed to have left that morning. He was short-tempered because he'd gotten himself involved in a situation that was none of his business—again!

"Bruno, you're making me ask a lot of questions because you're trying to be clever."

"He's killed a few men with his hands in fights, never with a gun . . . that I know of."

Clint released his shirt.

"Then why should I be worried about him?"

Clint drank his beer, ordered another. Suddenly—with him in his present condition—Rio had moved up to the top of the list.

# TWENTY

Even the other girls sensed that Clint had decided on Rio, and stayed away.

"Do you know what makes you interesting, señor?" she asked him.

"No," he said, "but if you tell me I'll do more of it."

She laughed and said, "No, no, it is that no one here knows who you are."

"That's good," he said. "I'd like to keep it that way."

"You will not tell me who you are?" she asked, moving closer to him. "Not even me?"

"All you need to know is that my name is Clint," he said, slipping an arm around her waist, "and that I want to take you back to my room with me tonight."

"You have chosen me?" she asked, blinking her eyes at him innocently. "From all these other beautiful women?"

"You know you're the most beautiful," he said, nuzzling her neck, "and most desirable."

"Of course I know that," she said, putting her hand on his chest. "I was wondering when you would realize it, Clint."

Suddenly, there was a crashing sound. Clint and Rio both looked up and saw the big man, Winston, stalking toward them. He had knocked over his table and chair in his haste.

"Oh, Lord," Clint heard Bruno say behind him.

"Friend of yours?" Clint asked Rio.

"No," she spat. "I hate him. He smells."

"So he's not your boyfriend?"

"I do not have a boyfriend, Clint," she said. "It is not a wise thing to have in my profession."

"You're probably right," he said, "for just this reason. You better stand aside."

He pushed her away from him just as Winston reached them, invading their space with not only his presence but—as she had said—with his smell.

Rio had understated the situation. The only thing Clint had ever come across that smelled this bad was a bear he had surprised in a cave one time in Minnesota.

"You got your hands on my woman, friend!" Winston bellowed.

Clint noticed that the center of the room had cleared out, patrons moving to the sides and the back, giving Winston room.

"Is that a fact?" Clint asked. "The lady tells me she's not your woman."

"Rio ain't got nothin' ta say about it," Winston told him.

He was even as big as the bear Clint had surprised, towering over him and the rest of the saloon.

At that moment Rio had something to say, though, and she said it in rapid-fire Spanish that Clint didn't understand.

"What'd she say?" he asked Winston.

"I toldja," the big man replied. "It don't matter."

"I said I would never have a smelly pig like you as my man," Rio told Winston.

The man looked at Rio, and, despite her insults, Clint

noticed that his expression softened. He was completely in love with the woman, and it didn't seem to matter that she didn't feel the same.

Under other circumstances, Clint might have stepped aside and allowed the two people to work things out for themselves, but he wasn't in that expansive a mood on this night.

"You heard her, big man," Clint said. "She's not interested."

Winston looked back at Clint and his expression changed again. It became dark, foreboding, and filled with hatred.

He pointed a huge forefinger at Clint.

"I'm gonna hurtcha."

"I don't think so," Clint said.

"Why?" Winston seemed honestly puzzled by Clint's reply.

"Because I won't let you."

"You ain't got nothin' ta say about it," Winston said. "I'm gonna hurtcha. It's as simple as that."

"No, my friend," Clint said. "You're the simple one."

"Simple?" He frowned again. "Are you callin' me stupid?"

"If you think I'm just going to stand here and allow you to hurt me, then yeah, you're stupid."

Winston looked Clint up and down and then said, "Gun or fists, friend. Your choice, but now I'm gonna hurtcha real bad!"

"Guns are used to kill people," Clint said. "Not hurt them. If you make me draw my gun, I'll kill you. I say the choice is yours."

That wasn't the first mistake he'd made that day.

# TWENTY-ONE

The other patrons in the saloon tried in vain to get even closer to the walls. They didn't want to get in the way of a bullet if there was gunplay, but they also didn't want to miss a punch if there was a fight. The stranger didn't look like he'd put up much of a fight against Winston, but there was no way of knowing how he'd fare with a gun against the big man. If anyone had taken a vote, it would have pretty much been a hundred percent for a fight and against gunplay.

Just in case there was a fight, some of them had already begun to make bets. Only the most ardent underdog lovers were giving the stranger a chance in a fistfight with Winston.

"You're givin' me the choice?" Winston asked, staring at Clint in disbelief.

"That's right."

"You're crazy, mister," he said.

"Or drunk," Bruno said from behind Clint.

Clint thought the bartender was probably right. He was a little drunk. His best bet at this point would probably be

79

to walk out of the saloon, go back to his hotel, and go to bed—alone.

It was being alone that kept him from doing it, though. Miriam Taylor offering herself to him had gotten him started, but now there was the prospect of taking the fiery Rio to bed. And to do it, all he had to do was get by this big moron.

Winston's shirt was open almost to the waist, exposing a hairy chest. He was muscled, but he was big and raw-boned, probably got that way from years of hard work. His fighting skills probably depended entirely on his strength. He'd have speed, and no finesse.

His hands were big and thick-fingered. Clint doubted the man could get his gun out of his holster the first try, and then when he did, it'd probably take him a while to get his thick index finger inside the trigger guard. He might have been accurate with the gun once he got it out, but he wouldn't be getting it out in a hurry.

All of these thoughts went racing through Clint's mind as Winston tried to make up his own mind.

"You kin walk on outta here, mister," the big man said. "No hard feelin's."

A collective groan went up in the room at the prospect of no fight at all.

"If I do, I'm taking Rio with me."

Now a sigh of relief went through the room. Something was going to happen after all.

"No, you ain't," Winston said, flexing his big fingers. "I tell you what. I don't wanna kill you. Not with a gun anyway."

"I don't want to kill you either."

"Well, then, I'm gonna take off my gun belt and hand it to Bruno there, behind the bar."

"I'll do the same."

Clint had taken on bigger men before, and come out

on top—though not without some pain. But maybe pain was what he needed right now. He needed to let out some frustration, and pounding on this big man seemed a fairly harmless way of doing it.

As they handed their gun belts to the bartender, Clint wondered if—when this was all over and done with—he'd even be in shape to walk out of the saloon, let alone take Rio with him to bed.

# TWENTY-TWO

The first punch, a looping right, whistled past Clint's head, and the breeze almost knocked him down. It also served to sober him up a bit—enough to realize that Winston himself was more than a little drunk.

The second punch was a left, and although Clint stepped back, it clipped his jaw, rattling his teeth and knocking him against the bar.

"He'd rather wrestle than box," Bruno said into his ear. "Don't let him get his arms around you."

"Thanks," Clint said, keeping his eyes on Winston, "but he seems to be doing okay."

Although Clint didn't need the help, Bruno put his hands on his shoulders and pushed. Winston opened his arms wide, intending to put Clint in a bear hug, but the intended victim ducked and moved past him.

Clint turned as Winston did, and he threw a left jab into the man's face. It hit him square, but Winston didn't even blink. Clint threw three more jabs in quick succession, all landing, and although Winston's bottom lip bled, he didn't seem fazed.

That's when Clint really knew he was in trouble.

Clint looked over at Rio to remind himself what he

was fighting for. He had to admit she was a magnificent sight. Her eyes were wide, her nostrils were flaring, and her breasts were threatening to spill out of the top of her peasant dress as she breathed heavily.

Winston came at Clint again, and was deceptively quick for a big man—not as quick as Clint, but he also had the benefit of a solid base. Clint figured what he might have to do was take the man's legs out from under him, so as Winston got close he kicked him in the shin.

"Ow!" Winston howled, hopping around on one foot. "You kicked me!"

Clint backed up and watched the man hop around and glare at him.

"You kicked me," he said again. "That ain't fair."

"What are you talking about, fair?" Clint asked. "You're trying to hurt me. Anything is fair."

"Not kickin'!"

"Anything."

"You sonofa—" Winston charged him again, and this time Clint kicked him in the other shin.

"Jesus, that hurts!"

Clint seemed to have found the big man's Achilles' heel, and it was his shins. That made sense. Most people's shins were tender. They certainly weren't meant to be kicked.

"You kick me again and I won't just hurtcha, I'll kill ya."

Clint wanted to find a quick way to end this, short of killing the big man. He saw his beer mug still sitting on the bar. The next time Winston charged him, he ducked him, got to the bar, and grabbed his mug. When he turned, the man was coming at him like a bull again, angered because of his sore shins. This time when Clint kicked him in the shin, he didn't stand and watch Winston hop around, he took advantage of it. While his opponent was holding his shin with both hands, Clint swung the mug and hit him right on the jaw, beer flying through the air.

Winston straightened up and stared at Clint. Blood suddenly blossomed on his jaw.

"You hit me with a glass?" he demanded.

Clint was about to do it again when Winston's eyes suddenly rolled up into his head. The big man keeled over and hit the floor with a loud thud.

"Is he dead?" somebody asked.

Another man leaned over and checked him.

"Nope," he announced, "he's just knocked cold."

Clint turned to the bartender. "Give me my gun."

He did so and Clint strapped it on.

"Now let me have a beer."

Bruno got him a beer and set it in front of him.

"You ain't got a scratch on you," the bartender said. "I ain't never seen nobody fight Winston and come out of it without a scratch."

"I got lucky."

"Mister," someone said, "you kicked him and hit him with a beer mug."

Clint turned to face the man. "What's your point?"

"Well . . . that just waren't blamed fair."

"That was as fair as it was going to get without me killing him," Clint said.

Rio sidled up next to him and slid her arm through his.

"Bruno, I am leaving early."

"No argument from me," the bartender said.

"Come, Señor Clint," she said. "You are the victor, and I am the prize."

Clint and Rio stepped over the prone form of Winston on their way out.

# TWENTY-THREE

When Sheriff Andy Taylor entered the saloon, the prone figure of Winston was still on the floor in front of the bar. Men were walking around him, drinking and ignoring him.

"What went on here?" Taylor asked Bruno.

"Stranger wanted to leave here with Rio," the bartender said. "Winston objected."

"And?"

"The stranger left with Rio."

"After doing this?"

"Yes, sir," Bruno said, "and it was slick as you please. Winston never laid a hand on him."

"Who was the stranger?"

"I never got his name," Bruno said, "but all the girls was buzzin' around him, until he picked Rio."

When the sheriff got around to talking to the blonde, Santana, she said, "I heard him tell Rio his name was Clint."

"Clint Adams," Taylor said.

"What?" Bruno asked. "Did you say Clint Adams? The Gunsmith?"

Someone else at the bar heard that and said aloud,

"You mean it was the Gunsmith who put Winston down? Hey." He turned to face the room. "That fella was the Gunsmith."

"Jesus," another man said, "he coulda shot Winston dead easy."

"Everybody calm down," Taylor said. "Nobody's shootin' nobody."

"Hey, Sheriff," Bruno said, "you oughta get the Gunsmith to help you when Ned Pine and his men get here."

"Hey, that sounds like a good idea," another man said.

"Why not?" Taylor replied. "I'm sure as hell not gettin' any help from any of you."

"Hey," a man said, "it's your job to face men like that, not ours."

"You got that right, Leo," Taylor said, recognizing the man as a do-nothing bigmouth. "Suppose you and some of your friends take Winston out of here and take him home. You can at least do that, can't you?"

"Yeah, sure, Sheriff," Leo said. "We'll take care of 'im."

Taylor turned to Bruno.

"Adams and Rio went to his hotel?"

"That's where they were headed when they left here," Bruno said.

Taylor nodded and left without a further word.

When they got back to his room, Clint and Rio frantically removed each other's clothes and fell onto the bed locked in a hot embrace. Hot mostly because the girl's skin burned like fire. The only heat that was more intense was the heat coming from her crotch. Clint placed his palm over her pubic thatch and swore it almost burned his skin.

"You must be a joy to have around on a cold winter's night," he said to her.

She laughed deep in her throat and said, "I can keep a man warm in the middle of a blizzard."

"I believe it," he said.

He rolled her onto her back and took her full breasts into his hands. Her nipples were dark brown, a perfect match for her dusky skin. Her long hair was black as coal, and if it was possible, her pubic hair was even blacker—and there was a lot of it.

"I like a full bush," he told her, wrapping it around his fingers.

"Sometimes I think I should shave it," she said with a sigh as his fingers probed her. "There are women who do that, you know."

"I vote no," he said, sliding his middle finger along her wet slit. "It's perfect just the way it is."

She arched her back as he continued to finger her. At the same time, he leaned over to kiss and lick her nipples, which grew turgid and chewable, so he obliged.

She reached between them to take hold of his swollen penis and press it to her hot and wet vagina. She was impatient for him inside her, so again he obliged the lady. He moved his hips and was inside her slick as you please, she was so wet and ready. And if her skin felt hot, and the outside of her sweet pussy hotter, the hottest place still was inside her.

Clint gathered her up by her buttocks and began to fuck her in long hard strokes. She gasped, wrapped her long legs around him, and bit down on his shoulder to keep from screaming. The pain from her bite drove him on, and he increased his tempo until he was slamming into her, banging the bedpost off the wall with each thrust.

# TWENTY-FOUR

Andy Taylor stopped in front of Clint Adams's room and pressed his ear to the door. He heard a thumping sound, and then two voices, both grunting and groaning with effort. He lifted his fist to knock, then hesitated. Finally, he turned and walked away. From the sound of it, Clint Adams was perfectly healthy, and probably happy. If anything, he wanted to keep Clint Adams happy.

He left the hotel and went home.

"He's what?" Miriam asked.

"In his room with one of the girls from the saloon," Taylor said. "Rio, the Mexican."

"A whore?"

"Not a whore," Taylor said. "A saloon girl. And she'll keep him busy all night, believe me. Uh, considering what I've heard about her."

But Miriam Taylor wasn't interested in how her husband knew about Rio's stamina. She was more concerned with the fact that Clint Adams had rejected her, and then gone out and gotten a whore. She hoped he ended up with a disease of some kind.

Taylor didn't notice his wife's distress, but therein lay

the problem with their marriage—one of the problems anyway.

"I'm going to bed," she told him.

"I'll be up in a while."

Miriam went to their bedroom, undressed, and got into bed. She thought about Clint Adams in bed with the saloon whore and felt herself becoming excited. If her husband had come into the room at that moment, and into their bed, she might have let him have her. As it was, she slid her hands down between her thighs to take care of the situation herself.

Damn Clint Adams, damn him, damn him, damn him . . .

In the parlor, Andy Taylor wondered what was in his future. He knew his marriage was in trouble, but that was not the problem that was tantamount in his mind. No, he could not deal with that until he knew if he was going to be alive beyond the next few days.

He poured himself a whiskey and carried it to the sofa. Hs sat and sipped it, pondering the problem. Sure, he had Clint Adams, the Gunsmith, on his side, but was that going to be enough?

Clint reached out and grabbed a handful of Rio's hair. He pulled back on it as he fucked her from behind, his penis sliding up between her thighs and into her steaming pussy. With every thrust, the sound of flesh slapping flesh filled the room as he bounced off the cushion of her buttocks. She supported herself on her hands, her head back, neck stretched as he kept hold of her hair.

She growled more than groaned each time he slammed into her, and as he pulled her hair she implored him, "Harder, harder," and he wasn't sure if she wanted him to fuck her harder, or pull harder on her hair . . . so he did both.

The line of her back was beautiful as it made its way down to the cleft between her ass cheeks. She looked back at him over her shoulder and her eyes were ablaze. She smiled at him and began to drive back into him, meeting his every thrust so that he drove into her as deeply as possible.

Abruptly, he withdrew from her, flipped her over onto her back. She protested at first, but then he dove down between her thighs headfirst. She was incredibly wet, her juices having soaked the sheets beneath them, and he wanted to taste her.

"God, you are a sweet-tasting woman," he told her as he licked her.

She was unable to answer. The touch of his tongue was like lightning striking her. She was struck speechless. She reached down to hold his head in place while he lapped at her. She lifted her knees to give him better access to her, and with her other hand gathered a handful of the sheets in her fist.

She'd never had a man be so concerned with her pleasure before his own. This was a rare man who had walked into the saloon tonight unexpectedly. He had fought for her—a fight that had, in itself, excited her tremendously—taken her back to his room, and given her more pleasure than she'd ever known. She was determined to enjoy every moment of it, and for the rest of the night make sure that he enjoyed it too.

If it was possible, she was going to make sure he couldn't walk out of the room.

# TWENTY-FIVE

Clint and the sheriff had made tentative plans to have breakfast together the next morning to discuss strategy. Rio had left before the sun came up—after they'd had sex over and over again—and when the knock came at his door, Clint wasn't sure his legs would take him there.

If history was any indicator, it was either the sheriff or his wife. He still took his gun with him, though, when he answered the door while wrapped in the bedsheet.

"Not interrupting anythin', am I?" Andy Taylor asked.

Clint looked around at his empty room and said, "No, you're not."

"Too early for breakfast?"

"Just give me a few minutes."

"There's a café down the street, serves a fair breakfast, although I wouldn't eat anything else there if I was you."

"I'll keep that in mind," Clint said. "I'll meet you there. Order me steak and eggs and lots of hot, strong coffee."

"Comin' up."

Clint closed the door and started to look around the room for his pants.

•  •  •

The smell of coffee hit him as he entered the small café. There were several tables taken, and in the back sat Sheriff Taylor.

"I thought you'd like an isolated table," the lawman said.

"Thanks," Clint said. "And thanks for this," he added, pouring himself a cup of coffee from the pot on the table.

"Long night?"

"Very long."

"I understand you had a run-in at the saloon."

Clint regarded Taylor over the rim of his coffee mug.

"You heard about that, huh?"

"I checked on Winston this morning," the sheriff said. "He's gonna be okay. You broke his jaw."

Clint winced. "I'm sorry about that," he said. "He pushed."

"I heard," Taylor said. "I came to your room last night, but it sounded like you were busy."

"I was occupied," Clint said. "What'd you want last night?"

"Just to check on you and make sure you were okay," the sheriff said.

"Well, I appreciate that, Sheriff."

A waiter came with two plates of steak and eggs and set them down in front of the men. At first bite Clint realized Taylor was right. The food was only fair, but the coffee was good and Clint ordered another pot.

"Your wife doesn't mind you going out for breakfast?" Clint asked.

"She's not cookin' me breakfast much these days," Taylor said.

"That right? Well, I guess there are problems in all marriages at one time or another."

"I'm not gonna worry about that unless I come out of this alive."

"Sounds like good logic to me."

Clint wondered if the sheriff knew that his wife had come to see him last night. There was nothing in his demeanor to indicate that he did, but who knew?

"What's on your mind for today?" Taylor asked.

"When's Pine due?"

"Tomorrow, I guess, or maybe the next day," Taylor said with a shrug. "No later."

"We better go around town and see if we can drum up some help."

"I've been all over town twice," the lawman said. "Nobody's interested."

"After my little set-to with Winston last night, I suppose folks know I'm in town?"

"Word's got around."

"Then maybe somebody will be willing to throw in with us," Clint said. "You know how people get when somebody with a reputation comes to town."

"Mostly, they either get scared or they try to get a look."

"Right. Also, somebody with a gun might want to impress me."

"Ain't no good gunhands in town that I know of."

"We don't need good," Clint said. "Just some bodies. If Pine and his men come to town and see a reception, it might change their minds."

"So we just need people who can hold guns and not necessarily shoot them?"

"Right."

"Well," Taylor said, "I guess we got our fair share of those in town, don't we?"

Clint nodded and said, "In every town."

# TWENTY-SIX

As they made the rounds, trying to recruit people, Clint recognized the attitudes and looks on people's faces. It wasn't their job to back the sheriff if he was going to face an outlaw or an outlaw gang. That was what they'd hired the man for.

Even when Clint and the sheriff approached the request from another angle—that once Ned Pine and his gang had killed the sheriff the town would be easy pickings for them—the answers were still the same.

Over a midday drink in a small saloon where nobody seemed to know who Clint was, he and Taylor tried to regroup.

They were sitting at a back table, nursing beers while Clint tried to get Taylor to come up with some more prospects, when the batwings swung inward and a man entered. Clint noticed him right away, knew the look. He wore his gun low on his right thigh, used his left hand to pay for a beer and to drink it, while his right sort of hovered around his gun. He was young, late twenties, a big man with deceptively slender fingers. He would not have the same problem pulling a gun that a big man like Winston would have had.

"You know him?" Clint asked.

Taylor turned in his chair to have a look.

"That's Joe Ransom."

"Ransom," Clint repeated. "I don't know the name."

"I wouldn't expect you to," Taylor said. "He's local. Grew up here, fancies himself a fast gun."

"Is he?"

"I don't know."

"Have you asked him for help?"

"No."

"Why not?"

"I didn't think he'd agree."

"Why not?"

"I told you he's local?"

"Yes."

"He and Ned Pine grew up together."

"Is he one of Pine's men?"

"No."

"Good friends?"

"Not that I know of," Taylor said. "But they grew up together. That usually means something."

"Maybe we ought to talk to him," Clint said, but as he said it, Ransom pushed away from the bar, picked up his mug, and carried it back to their table.

"Sheriff."

"Joe."

"Mind if I sit?"

"Nope," Taylor said. "This here's Clint Adams."

Ransom sat between the two men, looked at Clint.

"I heard you was in town," Ransom said. "You takin' up with the sheriff here?"

"He needs help," Clint said. "I thought I'd see what I could do."

"Heard you fellas was goin' around town lookin' for guns to back you."

"You interested?" Clint asked.

"We're lookin' for volunteers," Taylor said.

Ransom laughed. "The Gunsmith volunteered?"

"That's right," Clint said. "I don't hire my gun out, Ransom."

"Well, I do."

"That so?" Clint asked. "You're a big bad gunman, is that what you want me to believe?"

Ransom narrowed his eyes. Clint saw that he had hit a nerve. The man's next words were all bluster.

"I don't see as I got to prove myself to you," he snapped.

"Well," Clint said, "I'm not about to take your word for it, son. I know too many men who have earned the right to be as arrogant as you pretend to be."

"Pretend?" Ransom asked, pushing his chair back. "I ain't pretendin' nothin'. You want me to prove it here and now?"

"There's not gonna be any gunplay here, Joe," Taylor said. "You want to try to kill Mr. Adams here, you're gonna have to wait until I'm finished with him."

"That what you want to do, boy?" Clint asked. "Try me?"

"Why not?"

"Because many have tried before you and I'm still here," Clint said. "Why don't you try showing some real courage?"

"Whataya mean?"

"You got any reason not to stand against Ned Pine if he and his boys try to take this town?"

"Ned ain't comin' for the town," Ransom said, calming down. "He's comin' for *him*." He jerked his chin the sheriff's way.

"You think so?" Clint asked. "You don't think that after they kill the town's only lawman they won't decide to raze the town? It'll just be sitting here, ripe for the picking. You don't think your friend Pine is crazy enough to do that?"

"We ain't friends," Ransom said. "We just grew up together."

"So you're not out to be an outlaw like he is?"

"I don't got to be no outlaw," Ransom said. "I can make my money honest."

"With a gun?"

"That's right," Ransom said. "It's a talent, so why not use it?"

"That's what *I* say," Clint replied. "Why not use it? Stand with us, turn Pine and his boys away."

"For no money?"

Clint shrugged. "Who knows? After word gets around that you stood with the sheriff and me, there may be some money coming your way. Certainly a reputation of sorts."

Clint could see Ransom's mind working. A reputation after standing with the Gunsmith against a pack of outlaws out to take a town?

They had him.

# TWENTY-SEVEN

"How many other men do you have?" Ransom asked.

"None," Clint said.

"Just the three of us?" the younger man asked.

"That's right," Sheriff Taylor said.

"Against Pine and his men?" Ransom asked. "What's your strategy?"

"That's where you come in," Clint said.

"Whataya mean?"

"You know Pine."

"So?"

"Do you know any of the men riding with him?" Clint asked.

"I know his cousins."

"How many cousins?" Taylor asked.

Ransom thought for a moment, then said, "Four." He ticked them off on his fingers. "Rafe, Lew, Charlie, and Festus."

"Festus?" Clint asked. "What kind of name is that?"

"Old family name," Ransom said.

"Okay," Clint said. "Are any of these cousins good with a gun?"

"They all hunted as kids," Ransom said. "They can all shoot a rifle."

"And a handgun?"

Ransom shook his head. "Not so good."

"And Pine?"

"Pretty good with both rifle and handgun."

"As good as, say, you?" Clint asked.

"No," Ransom said, "I could always outshoot Ned."

"Well, that's good news," Clint said.

"I don't know," Ransom said.

"What?"

"The sheriff here," Ransom said. "I don't know if he can outshoot Ned—and from what I know, Ned wants him in the street."

"Don't worry about me," Taylor said. "You keep the rest of his gang from bushwhackin' me and I'll take care of Pine."

"So what do you say, Ransom?" Clint asked. "You in or out?"

"Are we gonna try to find some more men?" Ransom asked.

"Oh, yeah," Clint said. "We're not done lookin' yet. In fact, you can help there. Do you know anybody else who'd be interested in helping?"

"Not for free," Ransom said. "Come up with some money and I can probably get you two or three more guns."

"Good ones?" Clint asked.

"As good as Ned has."

Clint looked at Taylor. "That would put us at about a two-to-one disadvantage. Not bad odds."

"I don't have any money," Taylor said. "I live on a lawman's salary."

Clint gave it some thought. If he paid the men out of his own pocket, he'd not only be giving this situation his time, but his money as well. And he and Taylor and Ransom would have a better chance of coming out of this alive.

"If we pay them, would you want money too?" Clint asked Ransom. "I mean, it would only be fair."

"Naw," Ransom said. "I already said I was in."

"Actually," Clint said, "you didn't . . . yet."

"Well, I am," Ransom said. "The whole thing is starting to sound kinda interesting."

"Clint, I told you, I don't have any—"

"I'll pay them," Clint said.

"What?"

"As long as they don't want too much," Clint added, looking at Ransom.

"These fellas will take fifty dollars each."

"Really? How good could they be?" Clint asked.

"Like I said, as good as Ned's got."

"Okay," Clint said. "Okay, how long will it take you to rustle them up?"

"I can have them here by tonight."

"Good," Clint said. "Meet us back here at . . . eight."

"Eight o'clock," Ransom said. "Right."

He stood up, started to go, then stopped.

"One more thing."

"What's that?" Clint asked.

"You don't want to see me shoot?"

"You said you're good, right?"

"Right."

"Well," Clint said, "I'll take your word for it."

Ransom hesitated, then said, "Okay," and left.

"You really don't want to see him shoot first?" Taylor asked.

"Don't worry," Clint said, "we'll see him shoot."

"When?"

"When Ned Pine gets here."

# TWENTY-EIGHT

As they left the saloon, Taylor said, "I can't believe you're gonna spend your own money."

"Hey," Clint said, "as soon as I took a hand in this game, my life was at risk as much as yours. A few hundred dollars isn't so much when you think of it that way."

"I guess not."

"Let's work the part of town we haven't worked yet," Clint said. "Now we can say we have a few guns, maybe we can scare up a few more."

"Naw," Taylor said. "We're headin' for a bunch of storekeepers now."

"What about talking to the mayor?"

"He ain't gonna pick up a gun," Taylor said. "He's a politician through and through."

"Maybe we should let him know what we're doing," Clint said. "After all, he is the mayor, and he should know if his town's going to be shot up."

"You know," Taylor said, "I think that's a good idea. Let's go tell him his town's gonna be shot up and see what he does."

"Maybe he'll send for some federal marshals to help out," Clint said.

"May not be time for that," Taylor said, "but I'd at least like to scare his fat ass. City Hall's this way."

"That's ridiculous," Mayor Sam Bennett said.

He sat behind his desk, hadn't even bothered to stand up to shake hands with Clint. Of course, that might have been because he was wedged in behind his desk by his girth, which was considerable.

"What do you mean ridiculous?" Taylor asked. "I'm tellin' you, when Pine and his men get here, there's gonna be a war."

"Pine is an outlaw," Bennett said, "and he may be crazy, but this is his hometown. He's coming after you, Sheriff, not the whole town. I'd like to help you, I really would, but as I see it, this is your problem."

"I think you're looking at this totally wrong, Mayor," Clint said.

"Mr. Adams, I know your reputation," Bennett said. "What's your interest in this? Andy here can't be paying you, not on his salary."

"I'm just trying to help," Clint said. "I can't stand by and let a lawman get shot down."

"A fair fight." Bennett raised one pudgy forefinger to make his point. "Ned Pine said he wants Andy in a fair fight. As I see it, it's Andy's job to oblige him."

"You know," Clint said, "the sheriff can just pack up and leave town. What do you think would happen then?"

"I know what would happen then," Bennett said. "Pine would get here, find the sheriff gone, and go have something to eat, maybe visit some family. And we'd appoint a new sheriff, somebody who'd know better than to get Ned Pine mad at him."

"I was doin' my job," Andy Taylor said, "keepin' the peace."

"Pine and his men might have shot up some store windows, done a little damage that night, nothing we couldn't handle," Bennett said. "You went off half-cocked and tossed him in a cell. If he wasn't drunk, do you think you would have been able to do that? That's what got him so mad that he wants to face you while he's sober. Doesn't seem like such an unreasonable request to me."

"Are you really this naive?" Clint asked. "Do you really think Pine and his boys won't do worse than shoot up some windows?"

"Like I said," Bennett said. "He's a hometown boy. He lives here."

"He's an outlaw," Clint said. "He doesn't live anywhere."

"Mr. Adams," Bennett said, "what I would suggest is that you leave town and let the sheriff here do his job when Ned Pine gets here. I think that would be best for everyone concerned."

"I'm not leaving town, Mayor," Clint said. "You're going to see how wrong you are, and I want to be here when you do."

"I suppose we'll find out who's right and who's wrong when Ned Pine gets here then."

"I suppose we will," Clint said, and followed the sheriff outside.

On the street, he said, "He actually sounds like he's proud of Pine."

"Maybe he is," Taylor said.

"Why would that be?"

"Oh, I didn't tell you?" Taylor said. "The mayor is Ned's uncle."

# TWENTY-NINE

"I thought the *old* mayor was Ned's uncle," Clint said, confused.

"The old mayor is Ned's uncle on his father's side," Taylor said. "The present mayor is Ned's uncle on his mother's side."

"What are the two mayors to each other?"

"Brothers-in-law . . . I think."

"Okay," Clint said, "just tell me this—are you in any way related to any of them?"

"No," Taylor said. "I wasn't born here."

"Okay, that's good," Clint said. "I wouldn't want to get in the middle of a family feud."

"You're not."

"But wait . . . your wife."

"Also not born here."

"Okay," Clint said. "Let me take a breath. If Ransom comes up with two more men, we'll be five."

"Five against . . . at least twelve."

"That's not so bad," Clint said. "It would all depend on position."

"How?"

"Well, Pine wants you in the street," Clint said. "So we pick the street."

"Which one?"

"One that we can cover from rooftops," Clint said. "If we can get the whole gang in the street, then we can catch them from all sides. Then we'll have another thing on our side."

"What's that?"

"Two things," Clint said, correcting himself. "The element of surprise, and the fact that they won't know how many we are."

"That sounds good."

"There's just one thing."

"What's that?"

"Through all of this you'll have to be standing in the street—alone."

"Well," Taylor said, rubbing his jaw, "it's like the mayor said. It's my job."

"All right," Clint said. "We've got time before we have to meet Ransom. Let's try to scare up another man or two and, at the same time, show me a street that we can use."

"I'll think on it while we're walkin'," Taylor promised.

As Taylor had predicted, they did not come up with anyone else who wanted to help. They all had the same answer. "That's your job, isn't it, Sheriff?"

They had some supper—in a different café—and discussed other possibilities.

"What about your old deputies?" Clint asked. "The ones who quit. Think we can get them back with me involved?"

"I doubt it," Taylor said. "They were pretty scared when they heard what was gonna happen."

"What about some other young men in town?" Clint asked.

"Whataya mean by young?" Taylor asked.

"Seventeen, eighteen," Clint said, "even some kids we could use as lookouts. We're going to need some warning when Pine and his boys are approaching."

"We can get some boys," Taylor said, "as long we only use them as lookouts and don't expect them to handle a gun."

"No gunplay," Clint said, "but we can use all the help we can get."

"I know a couple of good boys," Taylor said. "Their mothers may not be thrilled, but *they* will."

"Good," Clint said. "We might as well check on Ransom and see what he got us."

They paid their bill and headed for the saloon.

As they entered, Clint saw that the place was not doing much business, even at what was considered peak hours for saloons. The larger places in town no doubt commanded most of the business. He liked the fact that he and the sheriff had the place largely to themselves, though.

Ransom was standing at the bar with two other men approximately his age. They did not stand with his confidence, though. There was more of a swagger in their demeanor that they had not yet earned. Other than those three and the bartender, there were only two other men, and both of their heads were drooping into their beer mugs as they sat at their tables.

As Clint and the sheriff entered, Ransom straightened and nudged both of the other men. They remained slouched at the bar, as if they didn't have a care in the world.

"Ransom," Taylor said.

"Sheriff," Ransom said, "Adams. This is Ed Kale, and that's Billy Delaney."

Now the two men straightened up. They were ignoring the sheriff, both looking at Clint.

"Boys, you know the sheriff," Ransom said. "And this is Clint Adams."

Now the men seemed to lose their arrogance and become a bit nervous.

"Mr. Adams," Kale said.

"Sir," Delaney said.

Clint looked at the sheriff, but the lawman seemed content to let him take the lead.

"I assume Joe has filled you in on what's going on?" Clint said.

"We know what's goin' on," Kale said. "Ned Pine's gonna kill the sheriff." Kale looked at Taylor. "No offense, Sheriff."

"None taken."

"He means to kill the sheriff," Clint corrected. "If he does it, we mean to see that he does it alone. Do you understand?"

"Sure," Delaney said. "You don't want any of Ned's men back-shootin' the sheriff."

"You got it right then," Clint said. "Get yourselves fresh beers and have a seat at a table. We'll be right with you to talk some strategy."

The two men eagerly accepted their fresh beers and walked to a table.

"Sit at one in the back," Ransom shouted, and they obeyed.

"Tell me about them," Clint said to Ransom.

"They're okay," Ransom said. "Not real good boys, but okay."

"Couldn't get anyone else?" Taylor asked.

"Nobody wanted to go against Pine and his boys," Ransom said, "not even with the Gunsmith. Oh, and I had to promise them a hundred dollars each."

"That's too much," Taylor said.

"It probably is, but it's fine," Clint said. "Can they hit what they shoot at?"

Ransom hesitated, and then said, "If it's not movin' around too much."

"Oh, great," Taylor said.

"Never mind," Clint said. "Let's just talk to them and see if they can take orders. Let's get some beers and join them."

"I got one," Ransom said, and walked over to sit with the men.

"This ain't good," Taylor said.

"Maybe not," Clint said, "but it's what we've got."

# THIRTY

The best thing Clint could think to say about Kale and Delaney was that they seemed willing and able to take orders.

"Get to bed early tonight," he told them. "We're going to be up bright and early tomorrow morning to get ourselves ready. As of tomorrow, Pine and his boys could ride in at any time."

"How we gonna know?" Kale asked.

"We're going to get some lookouts," Clint said.

"Who?" Delaney asked. "I didn't sign on to be no lookout. I want in on the action."

"The sheriff is going to take care of signing on the lookouts," Clint said. "You boys just make sure your guns are clean."

"I take care of my hardware," Kale said.

"Glad to hear it," Clint said. "Now get out of here and see to it."

"We'll see you in the morning," Taylor said. "First light, right in front of here."

"I got a question," Kale said as he and Delaney stood up.

"What's that?" Clint asked.

"Ransom here hired us on," he said, "but who's the ramrod of this outfit?"

117

"That's Sheriff Taylor," Clint said, pointing to the lawman. "What he says goes."

"Okay," Delaney said. "Just so we know."

The two men turned to leave, and at that moment the batwings swung in and a mountain entered. At least, it looked like a mountain and it blocked the entire doorway.

"Jesus," Kale said. "Winston."

Kale and Delaney looked at Clint. They'd heard about what had happened between him and the big man.

"He's carryin'," Delaney said.

"You boys just get out," Clint said. "We'll handle this."

Kale and Delaney had to turn sideways to get out the door, because Winston never moved. He just stood there, staring at Clint.

"What about you?" Clint asked Joe Ransom. "Want to leave?"

"I wanna stay," he said with a smile. "This should be interesting."

Taylor started to get up, but Clint said, "Stay seated, Sheriff. Don't spook him."

Taylor sat back down as Winston started over to their table. When he reached them, he ignored the sheriff and Ransom and stared at Clint.

"Winston," Clint said. "I want to apologize for last night. I had too much to drink—"

"Ain't got to apologize," the big man said. "You whipped me. My shins still hurt, and my jaw aches." He rubbed it. "Doc thinks it broke." He was talking with his jaw clenched. "I just think it's sore."

"Well, can you have a beer?" Clint asked.

"I heard you was lookin' for guns," the big man said, ignoring the question. "Gonna stand against Ned Pine and his gang."

"That's right."

"This all ya got?" he asked, indicating the other two men at the table.

"And the two who just left," Clint said. "Five in all."

"Well," Winston said, "I ain't got no feelings about Pine one way or the other, but I'd be proud to stand with ya, Mr. Adams."

"Why would you want to do that, Winston?"

"Ya whipped me," Winston said. "No man's ever done that before. And I didn't know who you was last night. Now I do, and it's an honor to be whipped by ya. So if you'll have me, I'd like ta stand with ya."

"It's up to the sheriff," Clint said. "He's in charge."

Winston looked at the sheriff.

"Hey, it's fine with me," Taylor said. "We can use all the guns we can find."

"Okay then," Clint said. "Do you want a beer?"

"Naw," the big man said, "I'm gonna go home and rest some."

"Okay, be back here in the morning at first light," Clint said. "Right out front."

"Yes, sir," Winston said. "I'll be here."

All three men watched him turn and walk out, and then the sheriff and Ransom stared at Clint.

"Well, if that don't beat all," Ransom said. "Ya whip him and now he wants to be your friend."

"It's a funny world. Ain't it?" Taylor asked.

"Well, we're six now," Clint said. "The odds are looking better all the time."

# THIRTY-ONE

Clint, Sheriff Taylor, and Joe Ransom had another beer together, and then the sheriff said he had to get home while he still had a wife.

"What about you?" Clint asked Ransom. "Got a wife waiting for you?"

"Naw," the younger man said, "nobody."

"How about getting us two more beers?"

"Too old and tired to go to the bar yourself?" Ransom asked.

"You got that right," Clint said, closing his eyes.

"I'll get 'em."

Ransom went to the bar, and the two men who had their heads hanging in their beers made their move.

Jerry Corbett and his silent partner, Carl Bankhead, had ridden into town that afternoon. It hadn't taken them long to spot Clint Adams walking the streets with a man wearing a badge. A couple of questions and they found out that Andy Taylor was sheriff of Cedar City. Neither of them had ever heard of him. Corbett had been expecting to run into the Gunsmith somewhere along the way, but this was a stroke of luck.

121

They watched the two men long enough to figure out that they preferred this little saloon to the larger ones in town. They'd also heard the talk around town about what had happened the night before when Clint Adams was in one of the bigger saloons.

"He'll want to stay out of trouble," Corbett told Bankhead.

"So what do we do?"

"We're gonna wait for him in his favorite little spot, and wait for him to make a fatal mistake."

Bankhead agreed. He was Corbett's "silent" partner because nobody knew about him—not even Tell Barlow. Everybody thought that Jerry Corbett did his jobs alone, and that was the way he wanted it.

They watched, giving the appearance of two men who were about to fall into their mugs, as one by one the other men left until, finally, Clint Adams was sitting at the table alone.

What the two gunmen didn't realize was that Joe Ransom was not leaving the saloon, he was just going up to the bar.

It wasn't Clint Adams who made a fatal mistake after all.

Ransom felt like having a whiskey with his beer. As he turned to ask Clint if he wanted one too, he saw the two men making their move. They took their heads out of their mugs and, without a hint of drunkenness, stood and drew their guns.

Ransom moved immediately.

"Clint!" he shouted, drawing his gun.

Clint heard the sound of chairs scraping the floor, then heard Ransom yell. For an instant he didn't know which way to look, and in that instant he knew he could have died—had it not been for Joe Ransom.

He turned to look at Ransom, saw that he was drawing his gun, saw where his eyes were trained, and knew he'd looked the wrong way. He immediately threw himself out of his chair and dove for the floor, clawing for his gun. Meanwhile, the sound of shots filled the air in the small saloon. . . .

Corbett saw Clint Adams hit the floor as he pulled the trigger, and knew he was going to miss. He saw his bullet gouge a hole in the table where Clint Adams had been sitting, then became aware of the other man at the bar, who had shouted. In his mind Adams had moved, and then the shout came. It was the way things happened sometimes—or seemed to—in the wrong order.

Whichever came first, he knew he was a goner. . . .

Joe Ransom drew his gun and fired in one quick move. His bullet caught Bankhead just under the chin as the man fired. His lifeless body was thrown backward across another table, where he came to rest. His gun dropped from his hand and hit the floor.

Ransom turned to the other man, who was just turning toward him. They fired at roughly the same time. . . .

As Corbett fired his gun at the meddler, Clint fired at him from the floor. His bullet hit the man square in the chest, so that when Corbett pulled his trigger his shot went wild. Then Ransom's bullet struck him, also in the chest, and he was dead before he hit the floor.

In seconds, it was over. . . .

# THIRTY-TWO

By the time Sheriff Taylor returned to the saloon—
having heard the shots from down the street—the shooting was over and Clint and Ransom had checked the two
men to be sure they were dead.

"What happened?" Taylor demanded.

"Those two threw down on Clint," Ransom said.
"They was gonna shoot him in the back."

"Ransom saved my ass," Clint said. He put his hand
out for the younger man to shake. "I guess I don't have to
wait any longer to find out if you can shoot. I'm much
obliged, Joe."

"Well," Ransom said, shaking Clint's hand, "I couldn't
let 'em shoot ya. We got too much to do."

"Who are these fellas?" Taylor asked.

"I don't know," Clint said. "I was just about to go
through their pockets."

Clint took out the contents of Jerry Corbett's pocket,
and Taylor fished around in the other man's.

"I got nothin'," the lawman said.

"I got something," Clint said.

"What?" Ransom asked.

Clint looked at both men and said, "A telegram."

"That mean somethin' to you?" Ransom asked.

"Yeah," Clint said. "Yeah, I'm afraid it does. Let's get this mess cleaned up and I'll tell you about it."

In the sheriff's office, Clint explained about the previous attempt on his life and the telegram he'd found in the pocket of one of the men.

"It was like this one," he finished. "Basically, hurry up and get it done, and signed by somebody named Tell in Selkirk, Arizona."

"Do you know this Tell fella?" Taylor asked.

"Never heard of him."

"Why is he lettin' you know where to find him?" Ransom asked.

"That's obvious," Clint said. "He wants me to find him. I'll know why when I do."

"And that's where you were headin' when we stopped you?" Taylor asked.

"That's right."

"I'm really sorry, Clint," Taylor said. "I had no idea—"

"That's okay," Clint said. "We're going to be done here in two days' time at most."

Taylor and Ransom looked at each other. Clint knew what they were thinking, that he was assuming he'd come out of the confrontation alive.

"I'm always looking ahead," he told them. "You can't ever assume you're not going to survive."

"I suppose you're right," Taylor said.

"You know," Ransom said, "Ned might have more than twelve men with him. We could be outnumbered more than two to one."

"We'll cross that bridge when we come to it," Clint said. "All we can do is get the men we do have ready. Andy, you were going to get us some lookouts."

"First thing tomorrow I'll line 'em up," the lawman promised.

"Um, you're not going to get any boys who are related to Pine, are you?"

"Don't worry about that," Taylor said. "We've pretty much gone through all his relatives."

"That's good."

"Except for the women," Ransom said.

Clint looked alarmed. "We're not going to have to deal with any of the women, are we?"

"Probably not," Taylor said.

"Unless they pick up guns," Ransom said.

"Jesus . . ."

"What do you want to do with the two men from tonight?" Taylor said.

"Bury them," Clint said. "I'll pay for it."

"You must have a lot of money," Ransom said, "payin' Kale and Delaney, and now payin' to bury these two."

"You know," Clint said, "even if I did have a lot of money—which I don't—I probably wouldn't after leaving this town."

"I'll talk to the undertaker," Taylor said.

"I'm gonna have a drink somewhere and turn in," Ransom said. He looked at Clint. "If you don't mind, I'll do it alone—just in case somebody else wants to take a shot at you. I had enough excitement for one night."

"Once again, thanks for the help," Clint said. "I might be dead if it wasn't for you."

"We all still might be dead," Ransom said. "Some of us ain't as confident as you are—but you're welcome."

# THIRTY-THREE

The next morning Clint met with Ransom, Kale, and Delaney in front of the small saloon. Sheriff Taylor came minutes later with two boys in tow who looked to be fourteen or fifteen.

"What are these boys here for?" Kale asked.

"They're going to be our lookouts," Clint said. He looked at Taylor. "Do we have two good rooftops to put them on?"

"Two two-story buildings at the north end of town," Taylor said.

"What about the south end?"

"They won't be comin' from the south," the lawman said.

"Who says?" asked Clint.

"Well . . ."

"I don't think we need two lookouts at the same end of town. Do you, Sheriff?"

"I guess not. Okay, so one at the north end and one at the south." Taylor looked at the boys. "You fellas work out who goes where."

"Do we get guns?" one of them asked.

"What's your name?" Clint asked.

"I'm Roscoe," the boy said.

"And I'm Marty."

"What would you boys do with guns?" Clint asked.

"Kill us some outlaws," Roscoe said eagerly.

"Have either of you ever fired a gun?"

"No," Roscoe said.

"Well, no," Marty admitted.

"Come here," he said to Roscoe.

He took his gun out of his holster, turned the boy around, and put it in his hands.

"See the horse trough?"

"Yes, sir."

The trough was only two feet away.

"Fire the gun into the water."

"Right into the water?"

"Yes."

"It won't make a hole?"

"No."

Clint walked the boy right up to the trough.

"Cock it," he said, even though it didn't need to be cocked.

It took the boy three tries and he had to use both thumbs.

"Now fire it."

The boy pointed the gun at the water and pulled the trigger. The recoil knocked him on his ass and he dropped the gun, crying out.

"My wrists!"

Clint picked up the gun, reloaded it, and looked at Marty.

"You want a turn?"

Marty looked down at Roscoe, who was cradling his wrists.

"No, sir," he said.

"Good." He holstered the gun, then reached down and

lifted Roscoe to his feet. "By the time you cocked the gun, the outlaws would be gone. Do you still want one?"

Holding back tears, Roscoe said, "No, sir."

"Good, then you'll both be lookouts. Just sing out when you see a group of riders—or any rider—approaching town. Got it?"

"Yes, sir," Roscoe said.

"Yes," Marty said.

"I'll take them over," Taylor said.

As the sheriff walked away with the boys, Ransom said, "They've never fired a gun? I fired my first gun by the time I was ten."

"I was twelve," Kale said.

"Eleven," Delaney said.

"Kids today," Ransom said.

They all looked at Clint.

"I lived in the East," Clint said. "Didn't fire my first until I was fifteen."

"Really?" Ransom asked.

"Really. Joe, I need some suggestions for a good spot in town for an ambush."

"We're gonna ambush them?" he asked.

"No," Clint said, "we're just going to want them to think they've been ambushed." He looked at the others. "You boys got rifles?"

"Yes, sir," Kale said.

"Yes," Delaney echoed.

"Go and get them."

He looked at Ransom, who was holding his rifle.

"Gonna have to tell them everything," Ransom said.

"That's fine," Clint said. "Where's Winston?"

"I don't know," Ransom said. "He should've—"

At that moment, the big man came shambling into view, wearing his holster and carrying a rifle. His jaw had turned some interesting shades of purple and yellow.

"Winston," Clint said, "you okay?"

The big man nodded.

"Can you talk?"

He shook his head.

"Can you shoot?"

A nod.

"Okay," Clint said. "That's what's important." He looked at Ransom. "Joe? Ambush?"

"This way."

# THIRTY-FOUR

Ned Pine tossed the remainder of his coffee cup into the fire, then upended the pot too.

"Hey!" his cousin Rafe said. "I wanted some more of that."

"No more coffee," Pine said. "We're headin' back."

"To town?" Rafe asked.

"Yeah, to town, ya idiot," Ned Pine said. "Where do you think?"

"Why're we goin' back there, Ned?" Rafe said. "Ain't we got some banks ta hit?"

"Yeah, we got banks to hit," Ned said, "and we're gonna start with the Cedar City Bank."

Sitting on the other side of the fire was another cousin, Charlie.

"We're hittin' our hometown bank?" he asked. "I thought we wasn't gonna do that."

"What the hell," Ned said. "A bank's a bank."

"And what about that lawman?" a third cousin, Lew, asked.

"What about him?"

"Ain'tcha gonna kill 'im?" Festus asked. "Ya said you was gonna kill 'im."

"Yeah, I said I was gonna kill 'im, and I am," Ned said, "but we're also gonna take the bank."

"At the same time?" Rafe asked.

"The sheriff'll be busy, won't he?" Ned asked.

"Yeah," Festus said, "busy gettin' dead."

"So," Lew asked, "are we goin' back ta kill the sheriff or rob the bank?"

"Both," Ned said. "I'm gonna kill the sheriff, and you boys are gonna take the bank."

"Ain't Pa gonna be mad?" Rafe asked. His pa was the present mayor, Sam Bennett. His brother was Lew.

"Yeah," Charlie said, "my pa won't be too happy neither." His pa was the former mayor, Charles Wentworth. His brother was Festus. Their uncle, Ned's pa, Tom, had been dead ten years.

"I don't care what either of my uncles think," Ned Pine said. "If you fellas are worried about your pas bein' mad, then I don't need you in this gang."

"I ain't worried," Charlie said.

"Me neither," Lew said.

"Me neither," Festus said, "but . . ."

"But what?" Ned asked.

"Well, what about our mas?"

All their mothers were still alive and living in town. Ned's ma had died soon after his pa.

"If you're worried about what your mommies think," Ned said, "I have even less use for you. You fellas wanna rob banks or not?"

"That's what we been waitin' ta do," Rafe said, "since you first told us about it."

"Okay then," Ned said. "Break camp and saddle your horses. We're headin' back to Cedar City. We'll be there before dark." He looked over at the second campfire, where the rest of the men—not part of the family—were hunkered down. "I'll go and tell the rest of them."

"We really need them?" Rafe asked. "We're gonna have ta split the money with 'em."

"*We* split the money," Ned said. "We're family. They're hired help. They just get paid."

Ned walked away from the fire.

"Finally," Rafe said to his cousins and brother, "we can stop wastin' time in these tiny towns around here and get somethin' done."

"Yeah," Lew said to Rafe, "but Ma's gonna be real mad."

"Ned's right," Rafe said. "We can't worry about what Pa and Ma are gonna say. We got to make our own way."

"But . . . how are we gonna do this?" Charlie asked.

"Don't worry," Rafe said, looking over at Ned Pine, "Ned will tell us." He shrugged. "Ned always tells us."

# THIRTY-FIVE

"When Ned Pine calls you out," Clint said to Andy Taylor, "you pick the place."

"The square in front of City Hall."

"Right. Ransom will be on the City Hall roof. Kale and Delaney will be across the street. Winston's going to be on the ground in front of City Hall."

"Why on the ground?"

"He can make use of his strength there," Clint said. "We don't know how he shoots."

"I heard he's pretty good."

"We'll find out, I guess."

"And where are you gonna be?"

"I'll be on the ground too. Watching your back," Clint said.

They were sitting in Taylor's office, drinking coffee. It was midday, the boys were on watch, and Ransom and the others were in the saloon, waiting for the word. They'd been instructed not to get drunk. That didn't affect Winston, since he didn't seem to be able to open his mouth, but Ransom said he'd watch the other two.

"You know," Taylor said, "if Pine finds out you're here, he might come after you when he's, uh, finished with me."

"Andy," Clint asked, "do you think you can take Pine in a gunfight?"

"There was a time. . . ." Taylor began, but then stopped. "I'm not sure, Clint."

"But you're willing to step into the street with him anyway?"

"It's my job."

"Maybe," Clint said, "if Pine finds out I'm here, he'll want to try me first."

"You'd do that?" Taylor asked. "For me?"

Clint shrugged. "It would be up to Ned Pine, Sheriff."

Clint and Taylor spent the afternoon in the office, playing two-handed poker for bullets.

Ransom, Kale, Delaney, and Winston were in the saloon playing poker for matchsticks.

Miriam Taylor remained at home, waiting for the sound of shots.

The boys, Marty and Roscoe, kept their eyes peeled, watching for dust clouds as they had been instructed, or simply watching for riders. At first sight, they were to run to the jail and tell Clint and Taylor.

Ned Pine had thirteen men riding behind him—his four cousins, who expected to be equal partners in what they took out of the bank, and nine other men who were working for pay. Ned had pretty much decided to kill the sheriff in town just to cover up the bank robbery. Originally, it was because his ego had been bruised when the man tossed him in jail, but Ned had decided his ego was not so important. Money was, and if it could be accompanied by a reputation for, say, killing a lawman, all well and good.

He also wanted to rob the bank to get back at both of his uncles—the former mayor and the present mayor.

Both had taken him in at some time in his young life, and both had treated him badly because his father was the so-called "black sheep" of the family. Well, to Ned Pine, "black sheep" meant that his pa was the one with *cojones* and imagination.

He was going to make damn sure he took every red cent out of the bank, and that both men knew it was him doing it.

But first, Sheriff Andy Taylor had to be taken care of. Ned had said he was going to kill the lawman, and he had to make sure he had a reputation as a man who did what he said he was going to do.

"We'll cover our faces with masks," Rafe said to his three cousins.

They were riding four abreast behind Ned, while the rest of the men were strung out behind them.

"They'll never know it's us," Lew said.

"You fellas are idiots," Charlie said.

"Yeah," Festus said. "As soon as people see Ned, they're gonna know it's us. There ain't no way to keep your ma and pa or our ma and pa from knowing that it's us robbing the bank."

"At least we won't be the ones killin' the sheriff," Charlie said. "That's gonna be Ned."

"Yeah, but we're supposed to help him with that," Rafe said.

"Maybe," Charlie said. "Only if Ned runs into any trouble. Personally, I think ol' Ned can take the sheriff all by hisself."

"And what about deputies?" Rafe asked.

"Forget about them," Festus said. "They done up and quit before we even left town. Ain't nobody in town gonna stand with the sheriff against Ned. That man's as good as dead."

"Hey," Rafe said, "what about his wife? That's a fine-lookin' woman who's gonna be left all alone."

"Maybe we can stop in and see her before we leave town," Festus suggested.

"And do what?" Lew asked.

"Make her a happy woman," Festus said. "Give her some lovin'."

"You mean rape?" Charlie asked. "I ain't gonna rape nobody."

"It won't be rape," Festus said. "Not after I'm done with her. She'll be beggin' for it."

"Says you," Rafe told his cousin. "Wait until she sees what I got for her."

"Okay," Charlie said. "I'll rob the bank and screw the sheriff's wife, but I ain't killin' nobody."

"Why not?" Rafe asked.

"My ma'd skin me good if I did that."

# THIRTY-SIX

One of the advantages of having the young boys on the rooftops as lookouts was getting to use their young eyes. Roscoe thought he saw something, squinted, and kept staring until he was sure. It was a dust cloud. Clint Adams had told him that a large dust cloud could be an indication that a large group of riders was approaching. Clint also told him that if he saw such a dust cloud, he should try to see beneath it. Sure enough, as he watched, he was able to see a group of riders just beneath the cloud. It was their horses that were kicking it all up.

This was it.

He turned to run from the roof, then remembered one last thing Clint had told him. He'd told him to try and get a count of how many riders there were. No one expected him to get an exact count, but Clint wanted to have some idea of how many riders to expect.

Roscoe squinted, tried to count, then when he felt fairly sure he could tell Clint there were at least a dozen riders coming, he turned and ran for the roof hatch.

The door to the office slammed open and Roscoe came running in.

"They're comin'," he announced breathlessly.

Clint and Taylor both jumped to their feet. Taylor dropped his cards on the table. Four kings, best hand he'd had all day. He hoped it was an omen of good things to come.

Clint grabbed Roscoe by his shoulders while Taylor broke out the rifles and shotguns from the gun rack. He leaned down and looked the boy in the eyes.

"How many?" Clint asked.

"I done like you tol' me, Mr. Adams," Roscoe said. "I looked for the dust cloud, I looked underneath . . . I done what you tol' me. . . ."

"Okay, calm down, Roscoe," Clint said. "Take a breath. How many?"

"A dozen easy, maybe more."

"Okay," Clint said, "go to the saloon and tell the others."

"Take these." Taylor gave the boy two rifles. "Give them to Kale and Delaney."

Clint had checked the men's rifles, and they would have been lucky not to have them explode in their hands.

"Tell them to get into position."

Roscoe cradled the rifles in his arms.

"Yessir."

"And then go get Marty off that other roof," Clint said.

"Then what do we do?"

Clint straightened.

"Then you both get off the streets."

Clint and Taylor both ran to the north end of town and spotted the riders.

"Gotta be them," Taylor said.

"Who else would it be?" Clint asked. "Are you ready?"

Taylor dried his palms on his thighs.

"Ready as I'll ever be."

"I'll be waiting in the alley next to City Hall," Clint said. "Good luck."

"You too."

Clint left the sheriff there to greet the riders, hoping that things went as planned.

# THIRTY-SEVEN

Ned Pine saw the solitary man standing at the edge of town on Main Street, legs spread, sun glinting off the badge on his chest.

"Who's that?" Rafe asked, riding up alongside him.

"That's the sheriff."

"He's waitin' for us?"

"Yup."

"That ain't good."

"It don't matter."

"But how did he know we was comin', Ned?" Rafe asked anxiously.

"Don't be stupid, Rafe," Ned said. "I told him we were comin' back, remember?"

"Yeah . . . but you didn't tell him when . . . exactly."

Charlie came riding up on Ned's other side.

"Why don't we ride right over him?" he suggested. "That'd take care of him good."

"That ain't what we're gonna do," Ned said. "Pass the word. Nobody talks but me. Got it?"

"Yeah, Ned," Charlie said, "we got it."

"And the bank closes in one hour," Pine said.

"You all know what you're supposed to do?"

"We got it, Ned," Rafe said. "We got it."

Andy Taylor stood his ground as the gang of men rode up to him, Ned Pine at the front. For a moment he thought they might try to ride right over him, but finally they reined in their mounts and sat there looking at him.

"Sheriff," Ned Pine said.

"Ned," Taylor said.

"I came back, like I said I would."

"I see," Taylor said. "Brought a lot of fellas with you, didn't you?"

"These boys?" Ned asked. "They're just friends of mine. They got nothin' ta do with you and me. They're just gonna have a few drinks, get some rooms, and relax."

"That's fine," Taylor said. "Won't have any trouble as long as they watch themselves."

"Fine," Pine said. "Let 'em through, then we can finish our business."

Taylor wasn't sure this was the way it was supposed to go. He and Clint wanted Pine and his men all in the square in front of City Hall. If they split up . . .

"Sure, Ned, sure," Taylor said. "They can pass."

He stepped aside and the riders filed by, leaving a cloud of dust behind them. When the dust settled, it was just Sheriff Taylor and Ned Pine there.

Clint was waiting in front of City Hall, and was surprised when a string of riders went right by. He watched as they continued on down the street, toward the bank.

The bank.

Clint turned and ran over to where Winston was standing, looking miserable.

"Winston, get across the street and pull Delaney and Kale off the roof."

The big man frowned,

"The bank," Clint said, "those men are heading for the bank! I'll get Ransom. We've got to get over there."

Winston looked like he wanted to say something, but he couldn't open his mouth.

"Just go!" Clint shouted.

# THIRTY-EIGHT

"Why does it take thirteen men to rob a bank?" Ransom asked Clint.

"Maybe because Ned knew we'd notice them."

"He wants us to catch them at it?"

"I don't know," Clint said. "I'm just assuming that sending thirteen men to rob one bank is kind of obvious."

"So what do we do?" Kale asked. "There's five of us and thirteen of them."

"We have to move fast," Clint said. "They can't all get inside the bank, so we take the ones outside first, and then the ones inside."

"What if the ones inside grab hostages?" Delaney asked.

"We'll have to deal with that if it happens."

"And what about the sheriff?" Ransom asked. "He's facing Ned."

"He's going to have to do that alone," Clint said. "After all, it is his job."

"Okay," Ransom said, "so how do we do this?"

They were a block from the bank. Clint said, "I'm still thinking."

•  •  •

Pine sat his horse, stared down at the sheriff.

"I can step down and we can do this here," he said. "Or did you have someplace else in mind?"

Of course Taylor did have someplace else in mind, but that obviously was not going to work. He looked around, though, and it didn't appear that Pine had any backup. Was it really going to be *mano a mano*?

"Come ahead, Ned," Taylor said finally. "Step down and let's do this."

At the bank, the cousins dismounted and Rafe took charge.

"Zeke and Del, inside with us. The rest of you stay out here."

"What do we do out here?" one man asked.

"Hold the horses. Make sure they don't get skittish and run off."

Another man looked around and said, "This is pretty obvious, Rafe."

"It don't matter," Rafe said. "There's no law to speak of, and nobody else is gonna go against us. Ned's got it all figured. Just stay out here and wait—and keep a sharp eye out."

"For what?" the man asked. "You just told us—"

"Just stay here!"

Rafe led his cousins and the other two men into the bank, where they brandished their guns and he shouted, "This is a holdup!"

When they reached the bank, the scene was ridiculous. There were more than a dozen horses in front of the building, and people were clearing the streets.

"Wow," Ransom said, "this is . . ."

"I know," Clint said. "Look, there's about half a dozen of them outside holding the horses."

"That puts half a dozen inside." Ransom said.

"They figure Ned's keeping the sheriff busy and there's nobody else to oppose them."

"So we got a surprise for them," Kale said.

"Yes," Clint said, "and we have to spring it on them fast."

Clint decided they had to take the robbers inside and out at the same time.

"How do we do that?" Kale asked.

"Ransom and I are going inside through the back door," he said. "You three will stay out here and catch them in a cross fire. It's the same plan, different place." He pointed. "There are enough high buildings here. Get up high and as soon as you're in position, take them."

"We don't wait for some kind of a signal from you?" Kale asked.

"This has all gotta go fast, Kale," Clint said. "It might not even work. We have no time for signals. Get up high and start shooting."

Kale, Delaney, and Winston went off to find their high points.

"You and me, inside the bank," Ransom said, checking his gun.

Clint did the same. "You up for this?" he asked.

"Three-to-one odds?" Ransom asked. "We got them right where we want 'em."

Clint smiled and said, "Yeah, you're ready."

# THIRTY-NINE

Pine dismounted, dropped his reins, and pushed his horse away. The animal trotted off about twenty feet before stopping.

"You look surprised, Sheriff," Pine said. "Did you think I'd bring help for this?"

"I wasn't sure, Ned," Taylor said. "This will be my first time finding out if you have any courage or integrity."

"I don't know what that last one is," Pine said, "but I got courage. You're gonna find out."

Pine spread his legs, dropped his hand down near his gun. Taylor did the same.

"Count it off, Sheriff," Pine said. "We'll go on three."

Taylor was about to count when suddenly he heard the sound of shots from behind him in the distance—probably from the center of town. He didn't turn, just stared at Pine.

"That'd be my boys," Pine said, "takin' the bank while I keep you busy."

"You'd rob the bank in your own hometown?" Taylor asked. "Take money from your neighbors?"

"I hate this town, Sheriff," Pine said. "Today they're gonna find out just how much. And it all starts with you."

"Ned—"

Pine didn't wait for a count. He went for his gun. . . .

Clint and Ransom worked their way around to the rear of
the bank. As they were in the alley right alongside and almost at the rear, Ransom said, "Uh-oh."

"Uh-oh what?" Clint asked, turning to look at him. "I
hate uh-oh."

"Well, I just remembered," Ransom said.

"Remembered what?"

"Bank ain't got no back door."

"Jesus, now you remember?"

"Got a back window, though."

"How do you know this?"

"I was hired once as a guard," the younger man said.
"Didn't last long, but I know the layout."

"Where's the window lead to?"

"A back room."

"Will they hear us if we break the window?"

"They might," Ransom said. "Depends on how much
noise they're makin'."

"Okay," Clint said, "let's keep going."

Inside the bank, Zeke and Del had the employees back
against a wall while the cousins were going from window
to window, emptying cash drawers.

"What about the safe?" Lew asked. "Ned said to make
sure and get the safe."

"Get the manager and bring him over here," Rafe said.
"He'll open the safe for us."

"I wonder what's goin' on outside," Festus said.

"Nothin'," Rafe said. "If somethin' was wrong we'd
hear shootin'. Now let's get this thing done before—"

Rafe was cut off by the sound of shots from outside.

His brother, two cousins, and the two other men all looked at him, and then at each other.

"Shit," Rafe said.

Clint and Ransom reached the window of the back room in the bank.

"Why's this bank got a back room anyway?" Clint asked.

"It used to be a general store."

Clint looked at Ransom. "Is the door to this going to be locked?"

"More than likely," Ransom said. "Wouldn't be too smart to leave it unlocked."

Clint sighed, then said, "Let's try this window."

They couldn't budge it. It was either locked or stuck.

"We're going to have to break it," Clint said, "and hope they don't hear us inside."

"I'll do it," Ransom said.

"Why—"

"We don't have time to argue," Ransom said. "I've broken into places before, all right?"

With a sweeping gesture of his arm, Clint said, "Be my guest."

Ransom took out his gun and without bothering to reverse it, smashed the window low in one corner. Clint was surprised at how quiet it was. Ransom had made an opening just big enough to stick his hand in, unlock the window, and slide it open.

"You *have* done this before," Clint said, and they climbed in just as the shots sounded from the front.

Winston obeyed Clint's orders to the letter. Unfortunately, he was the first one to reach a rooftop because he simply moved faster than Kale and Delaney. As soon as he got to the roof, he made his way to the front, crouched down, sighted down the barrel of his rifle, picked out his target, and fired. He was very good with a rifle, so the man went down, killed by a head shot. The other men reacted immediately, produced their weapons, and started looking around for where the shot had come from. A couple of them mistakenly targeted a rooftop and began to fire. Winston took the opportunity to fire again, killing another man, but now they had him located and fired back. A hail of lead drove him down beneath the roof ledge, and he was virtually pinned down until Kale or Delaney could start firing.

Winston wondered when that would be.

Kale had chosen the wrong building and had found the roof hatch not only locked, but wedged shut. He had to run back down and find another building.

Delaney, in his haste to get to the roof, took a misstep, twisted his ankle, and was hobbled. Slowly, painfully, he continued his climb.

Clint and Ransom ran to the door of the back room that led to the bank itself as the shots from outside continued. As they'd figured, it was locked. They couldn't break it down with their shoulders because it opened inward, not out, so Clint backed up and fired two shots at the doorknob, shattering the lock.

The element of surprise gone, they rushed into the bank anyway.

Taylor reacted as soon as Pine's hand streaked to his weapon. The younger man was faster, of that there was no doubt, but Taylor was more accurate. Pine's first shot went wide, and even as he adjusted and began to squeeze off his second shot, Taylor killed him. Drilled him dead center in the chest. Pine's finger never pulled the trigger a second time.

Taylor turned and ran back toward the center of town as the barrage of shots from there continued.

# FORTY

Kale finally reached a rooftop, got to the front, and saw
the bank robbers all firing in the same direction. He had
no way of knowing who was pinned down, Delaney or
Winston, but it didn't matter. He raised his rifle and fired
as quickly as he could, successfully attracting the attention of some of the men on the street.

Winston moved in a crouch to another place on the roof,
stood up, and started firing again. He knew he had help
now, he could hear it, and could see the men on the street
turning in another direction. If the third man—Kale or
Delaney—joined in, he could see that they would successfully have the bank robbers trapped.

Delaney dragged his foot painfully to the edge of his
roof, gratefully sank down to one knee, thereby taking
the weight off his ankle, and joined the fray.

When Sheriff Taylor came within sight of the bank, he
saw the bank robbers shooting up at the rooftops. Somehow, Clint had gotten up onto the roofs with Ransom and

the others. It was a good move, but what about inside the
bank?

He figured he had to try to get into the bank while robbers on the street were engaged. It helped that there were
better than a dozen horses, but almost at once some of
them broke away and ran off down the street.

He drew his gun and waded in.

The men on the ground were taking the worst of it and
knew it. When some of the horses ran off loose, a few of
the men decided they'd had it. They tried to mount up on
the remaining horses and ride off, but were picked off
from above.

Taylor moved in closer, slid between two horses, barely
avoided being stepped on, and made it to the boardwalk.
As he did, one of the robbers spotted his badge, turned,
and pointed his rifle. Taylor fired, but as his bullet struck
the man in the chest, the bank robber's finger jerked the
trigger. The shot missed anything vital, but hit Taylor in
the right thigh. He staggered, almost fell, but kept his feet
and made for the front door of the bank.

Inside the bank, Clint and Ransom came out of the back
room, guns ready, but there was no action readily avail-
able. They were in a hallway, and it appeared that with all
the shooting outside, their arrival—breaking the glass,
shooting the door lock—had gone unnoticed.

"Come on, come on," someone was shouting, "get the
safe."

"Let's take what we got and get out," someone else said.

"Ned would kill us!"

"I'm thinkin' Ned set us up, Rafe. We gotta get outta
here!"

"Rafe's a cousin," Ransom said to Clint.

"Well, whatever he is, we've got to stop them."

"How?"

"Only one way."

Ransom stared at Clint.

"We just go," Clint said. "On three."

Ransom took a deep breath and said, "Okay, on three."

Clint said, "One . . . two . . ."

Taylor didn't have time to look in the front window to see what was happening inside. If he did that, there was a good chance he'd get a bullet in the back. One of the bank windows was already shattered. He was just going to have to burst in and do the best he could.

Another bullet smashed into a window as he opened the door and rushed in. . . .

As Clint and Ransom came running out of the hall into the bank, Clint saw Andy Taylor come bursting through the front door. All three of them had to take in the scene in an instant, see the employees against one wall, the two gunman watching them, and the four cousins behind the cages.

At the same time, Ned Pine's cousins saw the badge on Taylor's chest, which kept them from seeing Clint and Ransom, giving Clint and Ransom a much-needed advantage in the six-on-three situation.

"Law," Rafe shouted. "Kill 'im!"

The inside of the bank erupted in gunfire. . . .

# FORTY-ONE

Abruptly, the exchange of fire outside stopped.

Winston, Kale, and the limping Delaney all stood up and stared down at the street. It was littered with bodies— both human and equine, as some unfortunate horses had gotten caught in the hail of lead.

The three men waved at each other that each was okay, and then they heard the gunfire from inside the bank.

Winston and Kale ran for the hatches of their roofs, while Delaney dragged his bad ankle toward his, but they all knew they would be too late to help the others inside with whatever was happening there. . . .

Six-guns turned on Sheriff Taylor as he entered the bank. Clint and Ransom hastily began to fire, drawing some of the deadly attention to themselves. Unfortunately, in order to do that, they had to shoot some of the men in the back. It went against every fiber of Clint's being to do that, but he felt he had no choice in this situation.

Before the bank robbers knew what was happening, three of them were down. The bank employees had wisely dropped to the floor. Rafe and Lew turned to face Clint and

Ransom, while Charlie tried to gun the sheriff. Festus, Zeke, and Del were all dead.

A bullet struck Ransom in the left shoulder. He didn't know who had fired it, but he pulled the trigger of his own gun and sent Lew to join his relatives.

Clint felt a bullet zip past his right earlobe, but kept his concentration and shot Rafe in the chest.

Taylor, already limping from a bullet wound to the thigh, felt something bite him on the side, but managed to drill Charlie dead center, dropping him to the floor.

And it was deadly quiet, inside and out. . . .

When Winston and Kale reached the bank and entered, they saw Clint and Ransom lowering the sheriff to the floor. Around them were the bodies of the bank robbers. Bank employees were still against the wall, some standing, some sitting, all shaking.

"Is it over?" Kale asked.

"It is in here," Clint said. "Outside?"

"Done there too."

"Everybody okay?"

"I think so," Kale said. "Delaney's limpin', but he ain't shot." Kale peered out the window. "He's checkin' bodies outside."

"Okay," Clint said. "Let's check the ones in here. Winston. Go and get the doctor for the sheriff. He's been hit . . . twice."

They settled the lawman on the floor and holstered his gun for him.

"Make my wife happy," he said. "Tell me I'm gonna die."

"I almost feel bad, but you're not," Clint said. "You've got a bullet in your thigh, and one took a chunk out of your side and kept going."

"You ain't got enough lead in ya to kill ya," Ransom

said. He looked at Clint. "I'll help Kale check the bodies, but I think they're all dead."

"Me too."

Ransom started checking bodies. Clint looked at Taylor and asked, "Pine?"

"Dead," Taylor said. "He was quicker, but he missed."

"Yep, that's the way it happens sometimes," Clint said.

# FORTY-TWO

Clint knew there was a very good chance that whoever Tell was, he'd be gone from Selkirk by now. He was sure to have gotten word that the other two men had failed. The telegram found in each man's pocket had to be meant to bring Clint here. He didn't know why the other two men had been sent first, but he wanted to find out.

He rode Eclipse directly to the sheriff's office and dismounted. There was a wooden shingle on the door that had EVAN WOODSIDE, SHERIFF on it. He entered without knocking.

A man with a badge was just walking back in from the cell block as Clint entered. He was tall, with gray, thinning hair, but had a bushy mustache to compensate for it. He had a thousand wrinkles around each eye, and Clint was sure there was a story for each one. He had the air of a man who had worn a badge for a long time—maybe not this particular badge, but a tin star somewhere.

"Help ya?" he asked.

"My name's Clint Adams, Sheriff."

167

The lawman stopped and stared. There was recognition on his face, but nothing else. He'd seen and heard it all by now.

"I know your rep, Adams," he finally said. "What can I do for you?"

"I'm looking for a man called Tell."

"Tell? Tell what?"

"That I don't know," Clint said, "and I don't know if it's a proper name or a nickname."

"Tell," the sheriff said again. He walked to his desk and sat down, waved Clint to the wooden chair sitting opposite him.

"Don't know that I can help you with this," he said apologetically. "I can check my posters for you, but . . ." Neither of them thought that would be much help.

"I have these two telegrams," Clint said, taking them from his pocket. "They were both sent from here by a man who signed his name Tell."

Woodside took the telegrams and looked at them.

"These weren't sent to you."

"No, sir."

"And the men they were sent to?"

"Both are dead."

"By your hand?"

"Yes, sir, but they forced the issue."

"Not my business what brought it on," Woodside said, waving the explanation away with one hand. He looked at the telegrams again. "Okay, this name I know."

"Which one?"

"Newly Yates. Bad sort, hires his gun out. Was here in town some time ago."

"And the other name?"

"Jerry Corbett. Don't know him, but while Yates was here, he was seen in the company of two men."

"Corbett could have been one of them," Clint said.

"And this Tell you're lookin' for coulda been the other." Woodside handed the telegrams back. "According to the dates on those telegrams, your man may not even be here anymore."

"Oh, he's here."

"Waitin' for ya, ya think?"

"I can't think why else the telegrams would have been in the pockets of these two men," Clint said, tucking them away. "Yeah, I think he's here waiting for me."

"Well, do me a favor."

"What's that?"

"When you two face each other," Woodside said, "try to keep the property damage down."

# FORTY-THREE

Though Clint didn't need the suggestion, the sheriff advised that he talk to the telegraph operator.

"He might remember who sent them."

"Much obliged, Sheriff," Clint said anyway, and then the lawman gave him something useful.

"Talk to Terry Benson. He's the regular key operator, got a good memory for faces and names. Tell 'im I sent you over."

"I'll do it," Clint said. "Thanks."

He left the sheriff's office and walked Eclipse over to the telegraph office. His hope was that he'd find this fella Tell and take care of him without having to get a room at a hotel. He'd already given this matter too much of his time. He wanted to work fast this time.

He tied Eclipse off outside the office and went inside. A skinny fellow wearing a green visor was behind the desk with garters on his long sleeves. The office was empty but for him.

"Help ya?" he asked.

"Are you Terry?"

"That's me." Up close, Clint could see he was in his fifties, and was wiry rather than skinny. That meant he did not look frail. Frowning, Terry asked, "Why do you want to know?"

"Sheriff Woodside sent me over," Clint said. "He thought you might be able to help me."

"With what?"

"These telegrams." Clint took them from his pocket. "I wonder if you handled them, and if you did, if you remember the man who sent them?"

The clerk accepted the telegrams, unfolded them, and read them.

"I remember these," he said.

"You do? Do you remember who sent them?"

"That depends." The clerk handed them back nervously.

"On what?"

"On who you are."

"Why?"

"Because the man who sent those," Terry said, "told me he'd kill me unless I did exactly what he told me to do."

"Which was what?"

"Again," Terry said, "that depends on who you are."

"My name's Clint Adams."

"The Gunsmith?"

"That's right."

Suddenly, the man looked relieved. "Thank God."

"What's going on?"

"Look," Terry said, "you gotta kill this fella before he comes back to kill *me*."

"And who are we talking about?"

"Barlow," Terry said, "Will Barlow."

"I don't know the—"

"He goes by the name of Tell to his friends. That's why he signed the telegrams with that name."

"Well, that's who I'm looking for," Clint said. "Tell Barlow."

"Well, he told me that if you came in here asking questions, I was to answer them truthfully," Terry said. "If I didn't, he was going to kill me."

"Why?"

"I didn't ask him," Terry said. "So, are you gonna kill him?"

"That depends."

"On what?"

"On if I can find him."

"You'll find him," Terry said. "He'll be at the Five Aces."

"Saloon?"

"Yeah. Just off of Main Street, on First. You can't miss it."

"He doesn't want me to miss it, does he?"

"That's the impression I get," Terry said. "He thinks he's real good with that gun."

"Thanks for the information."

"Hey," the man said before Clint had a chance to go out the door.

"Yeah?"

"He can't possibly beat you, can he?"

Clint shrugged. "I guess we're going to find out."

He started out the door, then stopped of his own accord.

"Tell me something."

"What?"

"Why wouldn't the sheriff know about this man?"

"He doesn't know him as Tell," Terry said. "He knows him as Will Barlow. I only know about the other name because of the telegrams."

"And where does that other name come from?"

"Middle name," the clerk said. "His name is William Tell Barlow."

Clint nodded his thanks and left.

•  •  •

As soon as Clint Adams was gone, Terry Benson came around the counter, closed the door, put the CLOSED sign out, and left by way of the back door.

By using both side and back alleys, he'd be able to get to the Five Aces before the Gunsmith and warn Tell Barlow that the man was coming. This had also been part of his instructions from Barlow.

Terry Benson was not a brave man. Barlow's threats had been all it took to get him to cooperate. Once he tipped Barlow off to Clint Adams's arrival, he'd be done with the man. He only hoped that the Gunsmith would live up to his reputation and put William Tell Barlow in the ground.

The sheriff had been the lucky one. The only instructions he had received were to send Adams to Terry at the telegraph office. Poor Sheriff Woodside, after wearing a badge for forty years, had had to bend to Tell Barlow's threats as well or die. Benson knew this irked his friend Woodside, but the old man was not the lawman he once was.

And Terry Benson had never been a brave man.

So the stage was set. Benson and Woodside knew that Tell Barlow was a fast man with a gun who had never had the chance to prove it to them—until now.

They only hoped that his first chance would also be his last.

# FORTY-FOUR

William Tell Barlow sat in the Five Aces Saloon, as he had been doing since the day he'd heard of Jerry Corbett's death. As the last of the three alive, Tell had gone to the bank to collect the proceeds of their wager, but it was never about the money for Tell. It had been about bringing Clint Adams to him, which the telegrams he had sent each man had been designed to do. He'd concocted a rule that the two of them had to keep the correspondence on them in order to collect if they won, and they'd been so dense that it had worked. So he knew Clint Adams had found at least one, probably both, of the telegrams.

A man came rushing in from the back of the saloon. The bartender recognized the telegraph operator and knew the time had come. Now maybe somebody would kill Tell Barlow and get him out of his place so his regular customers would come back.

Barlow watched as Terry Benson approached his table.

"He's here, Mr. Barlow," Benson said.

"I figured he was, or you wouldn't be here. He on his way over?"

"Yes, sir."

"Good. Then get out. You're not of any use to me anymore. And tell the sheriff the same. I have no use for either of you."

"Then . . . you'll leave us alone?"

"I want both of you to leave town."

"W-what?"

"After I kill Adams," Barlow said, "I'm gonna come for both of you."

"B-but . . . why?" The telegraph operator was aghast.

"Because you're both weak," Barlow said. "After I kill Adams, this town is gonna be mine, and I have no use for weak men. So get out."

"Mr. Barlow, that ain't fai—"

"Out!"

And as Terry Benson ran for the back door, Barlow called out, "And tell the sheriff to leave his badge on his desk. It's mine now too."

Jesus, the bartender thought, the town would never be rid of him unless the Gunsmith could kill him. He touched the shotgun that was beneath the bar, but he didn't produce it. He hadn't done it up to now, and he still couldn't do it.

"Bartender!" Barlow called.

"Yes, sir?"

"Bring two cold beers."

"Comin' up."

"And then get out," Barlow said. "I want the place empty."

"Yes, sir."

The bartender brought the beers over.

"And get out of town," Barlow added. "This place is mine now."

The man thought about arguing, but what was the point? If Barlow managed to kill Clint Adams, there'd be no stopping him. The first thing he'd do was hang those signs he'd had them paint over at the hardware store, the ones he'd use to rename the town Barlow, Arizona.

After that, he would be right.

The whole shebang would be his.

As Clint walked to the Five Aces Saloon, he noticed that the streets were emptying out. It was as he figured. The sheriff, the telegraph operator, or both had tipped Barlow off that he was coming. Word had gotten out onto the street already.

The only question that remained now was whether or not Tell Barlow would have help, or would face him alone.

# FORTY-FIVE

When Clint entered the saloon, he saw the man sitting there alone with two beers, one in front of him and one across the table from him. Clint walked over and sat in front of the second beer.

"You've gone to a lot of trouble to get me here, Barlow," he said.

"Not really," Tell said. "Other people have gone to the trouble. All it's cost me is time."

Clint picked up the beer and drank it. It was still cold. He thought about asking if the sheriff or clerk had tipped Barlow off that he was in town, but decided it didn't matter.

"So, now that I'm here, what do we do?" Clint asked.

"I've got lots of big plans for this town," Tell said. "But first I have to kill you."

"Why?"

"Because then I'll have the rep," the other man said. "I'll rename the town after myself, sit back, and wait for fame and fortune."

"And the people in town will just stand for that?"

"For the most part I won't bother them. I'll get rid of the troubling ones."

"Like an over-the-hill sheriff and a scared telegraph clerk?"

"Exactly. Even this place will be mine. I'll own the town."

"And that all starts with killing me?"

"Exactly," Tell said. "Plus I made a few extra dollars from the bet."

"What bet?"

"Corbett, Yates, and I had a bet to see who could kill you."

"And you collected already?"

"As the only one alive, I had that right."

"So you could have walked away with the money."

"Why, Mr. Adams," Barlow said, "that wouldn't have been honest."

Clint drank half the beer and said, "Let's get to it. In here? Or on the street where people can see?"

"I think if I walk out of here alive, that'll be proof enough."

Both men stood up, didn't even move away from the table. Clint waited, watched his opponent.

"Don't you want to know anything about me?" Barlow asked. "How many men I've killed?"

"It doesn't matter," Clint said. "If you kill me, you kill me. If I kill you, my reputation won't be enhanced at all. I've got nothing to gain, or lose. I just want to get it over with."

"Should we count—"

"Just do it!" Clint snapped.

Barlow sprang into action, drew his gun smoothly, and brought it up quickly. He probably would have killed any other man he faced . . . except for one or two—and the Gunsmith.

Watch for

**TO REAP AND TO SOW**

311th novel in the exciting GUNSMITH series
from Jove

*Coming in November!*

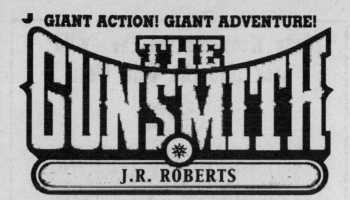

**GIANT ACTION! GIANT ADVENTURE!**

# THE GUNSMITH

J.R. ROBERTS

## LITTLE SURESHOT AND THE WILD WEST SHOW
## (GUNSMITH GIANT #9)
9780515138511

## DEAD WEIGHT
## (GUNSMITH GIANT #10)
9780515140286

## RED MOUNTAIN
## (GUNSMITH GIANT #11)
9780515142068

## THE KNIGHTS OF MISERY
## (GUNSMITH GIANT #12)
9780515143690

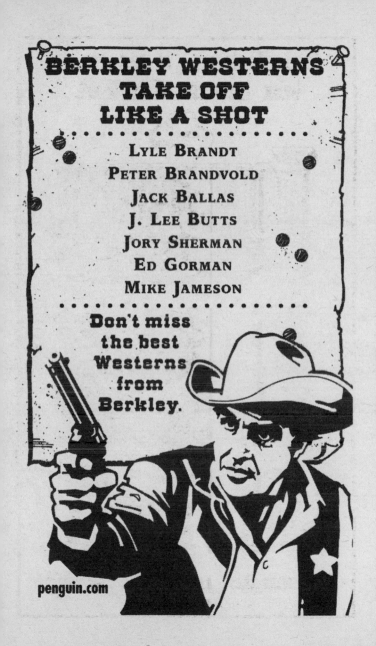